To: Jok

Enjoy this book prey
you are Blessed.

Love you

SCANDAL

SCANDAL

He who is without sin...

MARQUIS BOONE

MARQUIS BOONE
enterprises

Scandal

MBE books may be ordered through booksellers or by visiting www.marquisboone.com

Because of the nature of the Internet, any web address or links contained in this book may have changed since publication and may no longer be valid. The views expressed in this work are solely those of the author and do not necessarily reflect the views of the publisher, and the publisher herby disclaims any responsibility for them.

ISBN: 978-0-9887873-3-9 (paperback)
ISBN: 978-0-9887873-4-6 (ebook)

Printed in the United States of America

MBE Publishing rev. date: 08/28/2013

DEDICATION

This story is dedicated to every person who has ever found themselves struggling in their sin. It is dedicated to those who have been accused, forsaken, ostracized, and abandoned. May this book bring clarity, freedom and healing.

CONTENTS

Chapter 1 Lights, Camera, Action 9

Chapter 2 Nasty Vile Things...................... 25

Chapter 3 This Means War 45

Chapter 4 Army of Litigators 61

Chapter 5 Pictures 81

Chapter 6 The Mob 95

Chapter 7 Confession 105

Chapter 8 Witness Humiliation............... 117

Chapter 9 The Briefcase 133

Chapter 10 Money, Power, Respect.......... 151

Chapter 11 Fix It..................................... 163

Chapter 12 The Verdict 175

Final Word from the Author
About the Author

: S C A N D A L :

A scandal is a widely publicized allegation or set of allegations that damages (or tries to damage) the reputation of an institution, individual or creed. A scandal may be based on true or false allegations or a mixture of both.

What you are about to read is based on true events. If you are offended easily, this story may not be intended for you. **Read at your own discretion!**

Chapter 1

LIGHTS, CAMERA, ACTION

Eternity the Throne of Grace

"Valencia accepted her assignment as an intercessor. She has been lifting up the Judge from her divorce. Lorraine Allen is not a believer but the prayers of those around her have joined in with Valencia's. In her heart she desires to be good but she doesn't know she needs Us." The Son leaned back in His seat.

His Father nodded.

The voices of the Angels stopped. Heaviness replaced the sounds of worship. A stench never known on Earth permeated through the throne room.

A beautiful being appeared. "Lord."

"Where did you come from?" The Father said.

"Walking around on Earth and I want to take one of my souls to hell with me, Lorraine Allen." Satan smiled.

The Father looked at the Son.

"Father." The Son stood across from the enemy.

"I have a right to her soul. She's mine." Satan sneered at the Son.

The Father looked to the Son.

"There is no evidence she won't confess her belief in Me. Father, please, let Me stand in the gap for her life." The Son looked the enemy up and down. "Give Me time. If she knows how much We love her, she'll confess and then, her soul won't belong to him anymore."

The Father looked at the Son and Satan.

"Do whatever you want but don't touch her health or separate her soul from her body." The Father addressed the enemy.

The beautiful creature nodded. "Thank you, Lord."

The Son shook His head.

Satan left the throne room.

"You knew He was coming. That is why you told the Holy Spirit to intercede for her through Valencia." The Son sat in His seat.

The Father smiled. "You know what needs to be done."

The Son nodded. "We have to show her how much We love her."

"Her mind is closed to Us, so her heart is far. Send people to prepare her for You." The Father said. He looked past the clouds into her office. "She has no idea this is about to happen, her sins are unrepentant. Until she knows she can be free, we can't give her the life that You died for her to live."

"Thank you, Father."

Messenger angels stopped at the edge of the throne room.

The Father motioned for them to come forward.

"Master, there is a battle forming in Florida. We need help. The enemy has assembled a stronger army than I've seen in eons."

"The soul he wants has great influence on the Earth and he is determined to have possession of it and ruin any chances of her believing in how much We love her." The Father turned to the Son.

"Go and find everyone We know close to Lorraine Allen. She will need great intercessors to win this battle. Her soul is on the line." The Son said.

***

Monday Morning; Judge Allen's Chambers

Tick. Tock. Tick. Tock. Hands of the clock froze as the door to the chambers burst open. A camera with a light bright as the sun attached blinded Judge Allen, for a few moments. She raised her hand to shield her eyes. The bailiff emerged through the opposite door. A door that led to her cases for the morning, cases that required her to weigh both sides and find any truth about the matters brought before her bench. Truth that she wielded better than knight's of the round table swung swords.

A silhouette of a man's head loomed over her. A camera angled to capture every wrinkle, dyed gray hair, and nervous bead of sweat. Spittle gathered in the corner of her dry mouth. Tick. Tock. Time continued as the question from the faceless head registered. The smell of her own perfume filled her nostrils as her body temperature increased. Questions about her cabin in the mountains and her clerk being involved in less than acceptable behavior stilled her breath in its' passageway. Her eyes averted to the wall of books across from her desk.

"Judge Allen, is it true you've been involved in a salacious affair with your Court of Clerk? A convicted felon." His smooth baritone paused for effect. "Terry Johnson?"

Feeling rushed back into her extremities as she rose from her seat. Her arm extended and index finger flung itself toward the door they entered. "No comment. Remove yourself from my chambers at this instance before I have you thrown into jail."

Judge Allen locked eyes with her young, virile bailiff. They gulped at the same time. The reporter caught the interaction and instructed the camera operator to continue recording. "So you deny any inappropriate behavior between yourself and Terry Johnson? A convicted felon."

Blood rushed through Judge Allen's veins as she stepped from behind her large oak desk. Her shoulder's squared. Able to see the reporter's face she flashed her best diplomatic smile, waited a beat then exhaled. "Mr. Scott, I assure you I have no comment on this matter. Now please leave before I have you, and your entire crew thrown in prison for contempt of court. I have cases waiting and the public deserves prompt service."

The cameraman lowered his equipment. "You have what you need, I'm not going to jail. You're on your own in the clink. This equipment is my responsibility and I am not leaving it to the city to destroy, damage or lose."

"She's bluffing Maxwell, but you're right," Scott turned to Judge Allen and flashed a sinister smile. "We have more than enough footage and everything we need. By the time this is all over, the only one who'll be in jail is you, your honor."

Judge Allen felt every drip of poison from the way he said "your honor." She'd had enough exchanges with Scott and watched enough of his segments to know he was her worst nightmare. A reporter with a corporate ladder to climb. Hungry journalists were the bane of hardworking public figures. Journalists with reputations for ratings regardless of the damage caused or lives ruined were a menace she wished the law punished.

"Bailiff, show this gentleman and Scott out of my office please." Judge Allen nodded toward the door, again.

"My pleasure." The bailiff's well formed biceps flexed under his uniform. "You heard, Judge Allen, guys. Let's go."

Maxwell raised his free hand and carried his camera out like a precious baby in a carriage. Scott straightened his clothes and winked at Judge Allen. She recoiled and returned to her seat. The bailiff returned to the office a few moments later. He looked in the hallway and closed the door.

"What was that all about?" The bailiff said.

"Nelson, I have no idea. You know me better than that, Terry isn't even my type. Of course there is nothing going on with us." Judge Allen relaxed in her chair. "I want to know where that half plastic two bit gossip hound gets off accusing me of anything."

Nelson walked behind her chair and massaged her shoulders. His hands melted the knots of tension and stress from her body. It melted off as his hands slid down to her back and caressed the places he knew would help her prepare for their morning pre-court ritual. "Looks like you need this morning's briefing more than ever."

Nelson was good for more than securing her courtroom.

Judge Allen smiled.

***

Monday Mid Morning; Home of Terry Johnson

Maxwell hoisted the camera onto his shoulder. The weight of the machine gave him backaches and comfort. He loved his job, even when he had to follow fly by night failures like Scott. Catching Judge Allen with her robe up would be the only way his story would be good for more than a few minutes of filler on a slow news week. He picked up his steps to capture Terry Johnson exiting one of two doors from the address Scott insisted they rush to after their brush with incarceration.

"One of the doors is opening. Get ready, Max." Scott fluffed his perfect hair. "Be sure to get my good side this time. A few of those shots with Judge Allen her angles were better than mine."

"It's not my fault if that woman is built better than most women half her age and it shows even under that robe." Maxwell licked his lips.

"That is why we need to get all the dirt on her we can. She needs to be caught with her robe up and exposed for who she is, not who she pretends to be. I'm just the next primetime anchor to do it." Scott grinned as a tween boy dressed in sagging skinny jeans exited the front door.

Moments later Terry Johnson exited the same door. A waiting school bus opened a creaky door. Maxwell fixed the camera on Scott as he lifted the microphone and approached the other half of his ticket to the six o'clock news anchor desk.

"Terry Johnson…" Scott flashed a smile.

Terry's head ducked down and shoulders shrugged.

"…Scott Lovitt with Channel 3 News. I'm here regarding the scandalous affair you're engaged in with your boss, a pillar in the community and officer of the court, Lorraine Allen." Scott pushed the microphone in front of Terry's face.

Terry shoved Scott back while pushing the microphone away. "Get that thing out of my face, man and get off my property. I've got to get to work."

"We have it on good authority from a reliable source that you're the long hidden lover of Judge Lorraine Allen. We learned that you've even gone away with her for long weekends to her cabin in the mountains as recent as last month. Is that true?"

"No. What? No. Who would lie on someone as amazing as Judge Allen? She is more than a pillar in this community. She mentors children and so much other charity work. People have to beg her to borrow some of the time she volunteers. Get away from me before I bash your head into that camera." Terry took heavy steps toward Scott and Maxwell.

Maxwell thrusted his free hand out to keep Terry from coming closer to his equipment. "Scott, do something. I'm not explaining if something happens to this camera."

"No one is going to break your precious camera. Geesh, you treat it like it's a child. Just get these shots." Scott tried to intercept Terry on the way back to the car waiting before they attempted their impromptu interview. "We're going to release the information we have with or without your statement. It would be good to paint Judge Allen as the insatiable amoral woman she is so we can paint you as the harassed employee who was afraid of being fired."

"You're an idiot. Get off my driveway before you're a dead or injured idiot." Terry climbed into the car. The ignition cranked and engine started.

"That's my cue. I'll meet you in the van." Maxwell pressed some buttons and lowered the camera from his shoulder.

"C'mon man, we're trying to get a story." Scott shook his head.

"Go sit on your story." Terry flipped them off then pulled into the empty street.

***

Wednesday: Undisclosed Location

"Everything is on schedule. Her cases have been taken over by a sitting judge and soon the rest of her life will fall apart. As soon as the ethics committee finds the evidence we planted she'll be good as gone. Once she's gone we can get our girl in her seat." Scribner smiled.

"You're really enjoying this a little too much. It is beginning to look like a witch hunt. I wonder if you'd rather she be burned at the stake once you've destroyed her career." Blythe laughed. "Good thing we're past the days of lynching or she'd be in some real trouble."

"Lynching is too dignified for someone like her. Lorraine deserves something cruel, drawn out and humiliating. The evidence against her will show the world what an amoral, unscrupulous whore she is...sleeping with any and every kind of man ... Especially married men. All I have to do is plant a few more tips that are anonymous and leads and between the dismantling of her professional life and media coverage it'll be like a modern day stoning. When I'm done with her the only thing left will be a heap of bones and broken dreams."

"I'll make sure to never get on your bad side." Blythe cleared his throat.

"Good plan. Now I have the pictures from the last time meeting at her cabin. The investigator I hired was able to get a few incriminating shots of them at the cabin and around the courthouse. Once we leak those to the media and send the ones we doctored up to my office the Judge over her ethics hearing will have no choice but to remove her from the bench." Scribner leaned on the wall.

"Why are you sending pictures to your own office?" Blythe said.

"You hadn't heard...they selected me as Special Prosecutor over her case. I met with the committee head a few nights ago. We negotiated and once I agreed to her conditions and fulfilled all of her requests, she was happy to assign the case to my office." Scribner smiled. "I enjoyed it very much. You know how our meetings go, Senator. You also know how committed I am to my work in and outside of the courtroom. As I recall, you think I do my best work behind closed doors."

Senator Blythe cleared his throat again. "Yes, well, we can discuss our next negotiation at another time. I've got to meet my wife for lunch and contact everyone else helping us to take Lorraine down. Keep up the good work, Scribner, at this pace you'll be District Attorney by the end of the next election."

"You know me, Senator, I'm here to serve." Scribner pinched the Senator before they walked away from the corner the in corridor outside of his office in the State building.

***

Friday Morning: Judge Allen's Chambers

"Exclusive information from an anonymous source revealed that an ethics committee has convened to investigate Judge Lorraine Allen. An ethics clause in her contract as an appointed court officer means any proof of inappropriate behavior will result in immediate removal, possible fines, and termination and depending on what is found in the investigation, jail. Be sure to stay tuned to Channel 3 News as we continue to follow this story that we brought to you first two weeks ago." Scott Lovitt's lips moved and the word mute popped up in the corner of the television set.

"Do you know what this means, Lorraine?" Mark looked up from his desk. "They are about to sift through your life with a fine tooth comb. There is not a single thing you've done since you took office they won't use against you. I hope you have a great defense attorney because you're going to need it."

Lorraine leaned forward with a smile. "Of course, I have a great defense attorney. He and other's we know consider him to be the best. I've called in a few favors for him and he owes me big time."

Mark's eyes widened and his breath quickened. "If this were any other situation I'd love to work with you. You know how much I enjoy working in close quarters with you on special projects, Lorraine, but you know I can't help you. I've got a career, family, my son is in college and my wife is hell bent on being the Jones' everyone else emulates. Word is out that you've been put up on the chopping block; word in the circle has been passed around to distance ourselves. They're trying to make an example of you."

"Now they-- we know who's behind all of this. I'm not worried about what they say. I'll find a defense attorney outside of the circle if I have to, but I will not lose everything. I've worked as hard to get ahead as everyone else." Lorraine's hands shook. Her face turned red as she stood.

"My hands are tied, I'm sorry Lorraine." Mark stood and walked toward the door.

"That hasn't always been a bad thing when it involved the circle, but I see those times have changed." Lorraine looked Mark up and down. "Give your wife and children my best."

"No, I'll tell them you said hello. I'm selfish. I've always kept your best for myself." Mark nodded as Lorraine walked past him into the hallway of the courthouse. "Keep your head up, this could all blow over."

"If it doesn't they better be careful. I'm not the big bad wolf they're trying to paint me as, but I'm well equipped to blow someone's house down." Lorraine winked.

"Do you know any good lawyers outside of our circle?" Mark nodded at someone who walked down the hall behind Lorraine.

Lorraine shrugged. "I'm sure they aren't too hard to find."

A tall young man with striking looks and broad shoulders approached them. "Lorraine Allen?"

Mark eyed the young man and Lorraine.

"Who's asking?" Lorraine leaned on the wall near Mark's door.

"Tristan Reeves, I've heard the rumors circling around city hall and wanted to see if you'd secured a defense team for your trial." Tristan nodded at Mark.

"Look at that, Mark, I told you they won't be too hard to find." Lorraine smiled. "Okay, young man, I'm listening."

"Well, Judge Allen, I've followed your career for some time and I believe you're innocent. I'd love to work with your defense team to help prove that and get you back on the bench." Tristan said.

"I'm open to you being on my defense team. You're resourceful enough to know there is an investigation. Have you been able to find out who the judge on the case is yet? My connections haven't been able to pin down anyone we know." Lorraine sat on a bench next to the elevator.

"Sources tell me they're bringing in a special judge from the capitol due to the nature of the allegations and your connections with local officers of the court, someone named Joshua Light. I haven't heard much about him." Tristan cleared his throat. "I hope the lead counsel on the team doesn't mind my helping."

Lorraine stood. "I'm sure he won't. You're it."

Chapter 2

NASTY VILE THINGS

Eternity; Throne of Grace

The Son shifted in his seat. "Father, please don't allow the enemy to do this."

"He has legal grounds to disturb and destroy everything attached to her. She has never confessed You, look at all the sin. You can't get close to her until she worships or repents. When is the last time she worshipped You?" The Father said.

The Son dropped His head. He knew the Father only asked questions for the benefit of the person being asked. "Father, don't allow this to happen. Tristan's prayers are consistent. He is covered by My righteousness and chosen to advocate and intercede for His clients. Please grant his request. Help him win."

"Your intercession is accepted." The Father nodded.

"There are others, Father. Terry, Terrance, and Mrs. Johnson. Father, help them. Mrs. Johnson loves You very much and the ostracization of the others when Terry went to jail hurts her so much. She believes the church is all she has left. Help them." The Son said.

"As you request…" The Father turned to the angels waiting to approach Him.

"One more thing…" The Son cleared his throat. "Please release the hounds of heaven to chase her to the altar. Help her find her way to know Me. I'm going to knock on the door of her heart. I need permission to do whatever I need to do to show her how much I love her."

"It is so." The Father signaled for a different angel to come before the other angels waiting. "My Son has another request, whatever He says to do in regards to the battle for Lorraine Allen in Florida, make it happen."

"It's like we're one." The Son smiled. "Go and release confusion in the camp of the enemy. They are planning and plotting things to block Me from showing My love to her, work behind the scene on her behalf in the life of everyone connected to her, especially the Johnsons."

"Yes, Master." The angels disappeared.

"Well done, Son."

***

Tuesday Morning; Home of Terry Johnson

"Terry, I don't want to think about all those nasty vile things that unholy man on television says is happening between you and your boss, but we have to discuss what we're gonna do about Terrance." Mrs. Johnson sat in the chair across from Terry.

"I don't follow you." Terry's head felt heavy. Since the suspension, sleep was a distant memory. After the television reporter interrupted their lives, staying indoors or running errands at night were the only option.

"Doesn't it bother you what people are saying about you and Judge Allen?" Mrs. Johnson stood. She retrieved her favorite mug from the cuptree on the counter. With a fresh cup of coffee she returned to her seat. "I raised you better than being in and out of jail and sleeping with your boss. If you needed money, I have a little savings. You could have come to me. Now that boy is being teased and picked on at school because everyone saw you on the news. He can't take much more. His life was just becoming normal again before you were released."

"You tell me I can't come home without a job. I secure a job, while in prison so I can come home and raise my boy now you tell me I'm at fault because of something that isn't happening on my job. You're impossible to please." Terry's eyebrow twitched.

"Calm down. I'm not blaming you. I know you're trying. Those kids are picking at Terrance and teasing him. He has your temper; if they don't leave him be soon one of them is gonna get hurt." Mrs. Johnson lifted the cup to her lips.

"I'm home from work until this all blows over, maybe I can teach him." Terry's fingers strummed the table.

"That is ridiculous. He needs to be at school. You know how important it is for a boy to get a good education. Don't be selfish. You're loneliness is not cause for him to miss classes. Talk to him about what happened and encourage him not to follow in your footsteps or one of those kids is gonna get hurt and we'll have another jailbird." Mrs. Johnson shook her head. "I'm so glad your father is not here to see this, it would just break his heart."

Terry's head lowered. "Do you think there is someone down at your church that can help?"

"Help who? Some of them don't want to talk to me. I know they won't want to talk to Terrance or you. Give this some time to blow over before you start making any decisions, Terry. This family has been through enough due to you." Mrs. Johnson sighed. "I believe you didn't do it. Tired is all. If it ain't one thing here comes three others; we'll figure this out."

"Good to know you believe me. I know I've done things in the past but I've served my time, Mother. My debt was paid in full when I walked out of that prison. No one can claim I've done so much as walked down the wrong side of the street since I left that place." Terry stared out of the window. "I'd never do something that would send me back."

"I believe you and I know you're not interested in going back. Some way God is going to turn this all around, we just have to be strong for Terrance until we make it through." Mrs. Johnson leaned forward. "Is it possible this has something to do with ---you know who?"

Terry leaned forward. "Of course not. I don't deal with anyone from those days anymore. They don't have the kind of juice necessary to frame Judge Allen with the stuff their accusing her of doing -- us of doing. I'm not sure who's behind this but when I find out, they're going to pay."

"Terry, we just talked about Terrance not getting into trouble. Don't go do anything foolish either. Remember, you don't want to end up in prison again." Mrs. Johnson drained the contents of her coffee cup.

"One thing about going to federal prison you can't get anywhere is the education. Not my law clerk training. I'm talking about the education on how to be a better criminal. Street credit and tattoos are nothing compared to the lessons in getting away with crimes." Terry chuckled. "It's ridiculous."

"That doesn't make sense. They didn't get away with anything if you're talking to them in prison." Mrs. Johnson shook her head.

"It does if the person is convicted of tax fraud or larceny and is guilty of murder. I'd say that makes plenty of sense." Terry stood up from the table.

"Terry, don't do anything stupid." Mrs. Johnson called out as Terry attempted to exit the room. "Nothing is worth your freedom."

Terry turned around. "I know, Ma, but being locked up in the house with a child being harassed for something I didn't do isn't my idea of being free. Someone is breaking some laws; someone is going to lose everything they've worked hard to get. Someone is going to jail. That someone ain't me."

***

Thursday morning; Home of Judge Allen

Judge Lorraine Allen. The plaque on the mantel received from the youth center where she volunteered and mentored inner city youth gleamed in the sunlight streaming through a closed blind. No one remembered little Laney from the block, no one except Lorraine. Being accused of sleeping with someone she never would have dreamed of sleeping with made her laugh.

"This has to be some kind of bad dream. I'm being punked." Lorraine shook her head. The show about celebrities being pranked went off the air years ago. Nothing else made sense to her. She knew who was behind the attack on her character and attempt to remove her from the bench. What perplexed her was the why.

The doorbell rang.

Lorraine made hasty steps to the door.

The doorbell rang again.

Kenya tapped her foot on the porch.

Lorraine cracked the door open.

"Open this door, before I knock it down, Lorraine." Kenya's foot sped up.

"What are you doing here?" Lorraine walked away from the door.

Kenya entered the house. She closed and locked the front door. "There's no paparazzi outside so you can

31

open the blinds a little bit. Your house looks like a vampire lives here."

"Good to see you, too." Lorraine slumped down in her oversized vanilla leather chair. "What the hell are you doing here?"

"So you divorce my brother and I'm supposed to just walk away from my best friend? You've been distant over the last few years but I thought we were still friends, Lorraine." Kenya made herself comfortable on the loveseat across from the chair. "The real question is what the hell is going on with you?"

Lorraine felt her shoulders relax. Tension settled in the small of her back. The need to unburden her soul with someone she trusted filled her from head to toe but fear bridled her tongue. "You know I've been busy with work. Between court and charity work, I barely have time to get these gray hairs dyed. Enough about my boring life; how are my godchildren? Lizzy should be starting senior year of high school and Sean should be in his second year at University of Oklahoma."

"I'm not going to sit here and talk about stuff you can read about my life on Facebook. I saw the news report. Dyson saw the reports on the news. You may not be his wife anymore but he is still concerned about you. We all are, and for good reason. Sleeping with your clerk...Lorraine?" Kenya said.

Lorraine closed her eyes. She took in a deep breath. When she couldn't hold it any longer she released it. "Long as we've been friends and you had to ask if I did something like that. I thought you knew me."

"I do. That is why I'm here. You traded Dyson in to advance your career goals. I don't acknowledge the rumors I hear about the circles," Kenya put air quotes around the word circles, "you travel with but I'm no fool, Lorraine. I knew you before Dyson and I know you now. It doesn't surprise me that the bones are falling out of the closet. That is not why I'm here. I'm here to make sure you're okay."

Lorraine exhaled. Kenya held a special place in her heart because no matter what other's said about her Kenya refused to give up. Their friendship had been battered by bumbling boyfriends, jealous groupie girls trying to get with Dyson, a rocky relationship as sister-in-laws, a painful marriage and hard divorce. She never forgave herself for the way she treated Dyson in their relationship. The most eligible bachelor in their town fell in love with her and she fell in love with the law.

"Paging Lorraine..." Kenya snapped her fingers in front of Lorraine's face.

"Sorry," Lorraine offered a sad smile. "You know me better than anyone else; you know I didn't do this. I

33

wouldn't jeopardize my life's work for a few cheap thrills with my law clerk. Please."

Kenya leaned forward. "I know that, Lorraine, and I also know how much you hate being lied on. I'm here to make sure you're not plotting something stupid. This isn't high school and we're not beefing with some chicken-head girl who has Dyson in her crosshairs. You're being investigated for unethical practices and your entire life is being turned inside out. I need to know if you're going to recover or are they going to find something and destroy you with this?"

Lorraine rubbed her hands on the front of her pants. Leave it to her best friend to lay all the cards on the table while she wanted the dealer to give her a new hand. "I'm well aware of what I stand to lose if anything were to come out. There is nothing for them to find that won't bring this entire city and state to its knees."

Kenya sat back. "I hope you're right. The things I heard about you were a bit over the top but I know that secrets are what get people placed in positions of power in this government. You're an amazing lawyer and a great judge but questions about how you were appointed have swirled around since you were announced as a candidate."

Lorraine wrestled with the desire to tell Kenya the truth. Secrets, closed door deals and back-room propositions were the oil that kept the political machine running from the courtroom to the oval office. She wanted to tell her ex-husband's sister the truth but there was no way she could keep her last shred of dignity intact and be honest with the only person who'd supported her all her life. "I lost everything making my career dreams come true, Kenya. You know all the things I've sacrificed to get where I am. I'm telling you right here, right now, I didn't do what they're accusing me of. Terry isn't even my type."

"I know your type but ever since you decided to marry your career there have been a lot of things I thought I knew about you that changed. Call me if you need to talk." Kenya shrugged. She picked her purse up from the floor. Her steps were slow toward the front door. "A lot has changed between us over the years, Lorraine, but just know I'll always be here, if for nothing else as a listening ear. Don't do something stupid to fix this. Before you do anything, promise you'll call me."

A smile spread across Lorraine's face. Kenya filled so many roles in her life over time she wondered how a girl so close to her age knew when to be her sister, confidant, roll dawg and friend. In the moments when Kenya mothered her and took her best interest to heart, Kenya reminded Lorraine of why they branded the same heart and key tattoo in a place only those they loved would ever see. "I hear you, Kenya. Trust me; I'm not going to do anything hasty."

"Good. This is not a game, these people aren't playing with you, your life is something they want to take and keep." Kenya waited for Lorraine at the door. They shared a brief hug. As fast as she came she was gone. The weight of her secrets encircled her.

***

Undisclosed Location

Scribner sat down at the head of the table. Senator Blythe, Judge Carver, Alderman Holt, and Dr. Shields sat on opposite sides of the table. A folder full of papers sat in front of each person. Scribner opened the folder first. The air seemed to disappear from the room.

"Does anyone have any good news before we go over this information?" Scribner said.

Senator Blythe cleared his throat. A bead of sweat popped up on his brow.

Judge Carver fingered his collar.

Dr. Shields strummed his fingers on the table next to the folder.

Alderman Holt twiddled with his pen.

"There has to be more on this woman than you've been able to turn up. She is not this squeaky clean. No one is admitted into the circle we run with unless their hands are a little dirty. It's easier to keep someone in line with what we want them to do when their dirt can be uncovered without showing ours." Scribner's fist slammed down on the table. "Come on men. This is starting to make us look bad."

Dr. Shields' fingers froze mid strum. "There could be something in her medical records that incriminates her or makes her look shady. I can have some of my connections pull her information and see what we can dredge up."

"That is more of what I'm talking about, she is a part of our circle. I know she has to have something we can use against her." Scribner smiled.

"I've already turned over every contact in my district, between her mentoring and volunteering. They love her enough to erect a statue in her honor at the park she helped raise money to have built in place of the old Tarson building used as a drug house." Alderman Holt said.

"I have yet to visit a neighborhood without a hateful ol' busybody who found fault in something everyone did. Your community isn't exempt, find her and get the dirt on Judge Allen." Scribner turned to face Judge Carver. "Please explain to me how some random person none of us knows or has heard of has been assigned to our case."

"I didn't deliver the money to the head of the committee so I don't know anything about any payment. As far as being assigned the case, I won't have enough favors built up before I retire to be assigned to oversee the Chief Justice's protégé. He laughed at me before I attempted to be assigned to the case. The only thing we discussed was you being Special Prosecutor." Judge Carver stared at Scribner until they both looked away.

"We're not going to be able to make a case against her overnight or with the truth. You and everyone else here knows how squeaky clean, Lorraine likes to keep herself. That is one of the reason's we wanted her." Senator Blythe leaned forward and dropped his voice to just above a whisper. "The person Lorraine replaced was killed before she was the death of all our careers. Now you want to destroy one of the best legal minds we've seen since I joined the legal profession because she won't play nice with you. I hope you know what you're doing, Scribner. If this backfires we'll all have to find new professions. I'm not interested in starting over as a stock boy at Walmart in my fifties."

"Don't get your boxers in a ball, Walter. You'll be able to ride out your cushy job in Congress another two or three terms unless the constituents you represent wake up with their heads removed from their pretentious backsides. You just keep working your connections and use some of that power to dig something up in her past. No one is as clean as she is, who does the things you all know she does, behind closed doors. Someone knows something, find them and get them to spill it." Scribner looked through the information in the file in front of her. "I refuse to believe anyone who does the things we know she'll do, doesn't do anything else on the wrong side of the morality line. I've never heard of anything more absurd. If we don't find anything soon, we can always do the next best thing. Manufactured evidence ruins defendants better than the real thing, in desperate situations."

***

Lorraine took cautious steps toward the door. She'd checked it twice and found the porch empty. Embarrassment over her jumbled nerves filled her belly. A peek through the curtains revealed Tristan looking for her misplaced bell.

"It's next to the bottom of the mailbox. You can't see it unless you know it's there." Lorraine smiled. "Come on in. Join me for something to drink in the kitchen. There is lemonade, soda and bottled water. Too early in the day for alcohol for most, but I won't tell anyone if you don't."

"Lemonade is fine." Tristan appeared nervous as he crossed her threshold. "Need to wash my hands. Bathroom?"

"Second door on the left." Lorraine pointed toward a dark room with a door half open next to a closed door. "Make a left out of the bathroom and it'll lead you into the kitchen."

Tristan nodded.

A formal drink setting waited for Lorraine on her bright eat-in kitchen table. Moments later Tristan walked into the opening in front of the table. The light from her laptop screen reflected off the window.

"Help yourself, the lemonade is chilled but the bucket has cubed ice as well." Lorraine imagined them in the coziness of her cabin under different circumstances. "You have a thriving practice and have offered stellar counsel so far. How is it we don't travel in the same circles?"

"You practice family law and most of my clients are non profit entities, churches for the most part. My Pastor may have missed his true call as a marketer. He brings me more business than I can stand." Tristan cleared his throat and smiled.

"I may need him to help me get my private practice going again, if this doesn't work out. Even if it does, depending on what comes out, my time on the bench may be over." Lorraine shook her head. She dropped into her seat.

"Where is your faith, Lorraine? As soon as I heard the story I knew you were innocent. Tell me different and I'll believe it, but I knew in my gut you weren't having an affair with your clerk." Tristan pulled an iPad from his briefcase.

"You have an interesting way of picking cases. Gut instinct is good, and you're correct, I'm so used to being around people who want something for every favor. Forgive me for seeming a little closed. I still haven't figured you out. What is in this for you?" Lorraine shrugged.

"Obedience. When I saw your case, God placed it on my heart to represent you in whatever way you needed. No one could've convinced me you'd be without representation." Tristan shook his head. "The only thing in it for me is doing what I know God told me to do, and that is to get you back to work."

"Well, I'll be happy to pay your fee." Lorraine unzipped her leisure suit jacket so the top of her cleavage peeked out. "You're welcome to anything else you see that you like."

Tristan cleared his throat. He poured more lemonade in his half full glass.

"Have you found anything out about the judge?" Lorraine opened the folder next to her laptop. "I've tried to find something on him, but he is clean as a whistle. He came from nowhere, kinda like you did."

"Joshua Light, he is semi-retired and only sits on special litigation trials. My wife said she is related to some Lights two or three generations over but I'm sure it is a very common last name. He lives closer to the capitol, which may be why no one knows much about him." Tristan seemed to have regrouped. "Is there anything you want to tell me that will help with your defense?"

Lorraine shook her head no. She could never tell him about the circle she ran with, or what they did to help each other advance in their careers. To be rumored to engage in questionable behavior, then admit it to someone as pious and trusting as Tristan felt like a bad idea. The weight of her actions and regret about sacrificing the love of her life, friendships and part of her soul to succeed weighed on her more each day she sat home waiting for her trial.

"You're sure there is nothing I need to know, that may help the case? Is there anything about your past they could use to make you look like the kind of person who'd sleep with Terry? A convicted felon working in a court of law as a clerk looks suspicious. I'm familiar with the program that puts one time offenders back to work. Since most laypeople aren't aware of the program I think a bench trial will be in your best interest."

Lorraine smiled. Concern about the public's ignorance regarding the program that caused her to hire Terry was the least of her worries. Scribner and the invisible circle of Scribner's supporters offered the biggest threat to Lorraine's career she never imagined. The decorations, atmosphere and tone of their networking mixers bordered on Hedonistic. Tristan ignored all of her subtle advances. She refused to reveal the truth about her recent corporate ladder ascension. She nodded.

"Glad we're in agreement. The burden of proof is on the special prosecutor. You're innocent so short of doctoring evidence we'll be able to get this messy ordeal behind you." Tristan drained the contents of his glass. "My wife made me promise to be home at a decent hour today. Is there anything you can think of that I need to prepare for so I'm not sideswiped by any of the shenanigans Scribner is known to use?"

Lorraine shook her head.

"Ok, speak now or forever hold your peace." Tristan chuckled. "You have your outfit for tomorrow picked out?"

Lorraine nodded. "When do you want to prepare me for the witness stand?"

Tristan cleared his throat.

Lorraine stared at Tristan.

"It may be best for you not to take the witness stand. I'm sure you'll provide useful testimony for us but I've heard about the way Scribner's team uses testimony to make pretzels of witnesses before they leave the stand. Their mistrial before conviction record is legendary. Bench trial and no time on the witness stand is what I'd tell any other client in this predicament, and that is what I suggest to you." Tristan's shoulders relaxed.

Chapter 3

THIS MEANS WAR

Eternity: Throne of Grace

A war torn angel entered the throne room. The Son motioned for the angels and saints to stop singing. "Come."

The Father looked at them. "I've been expecting your report."

"We've attempted to infiltrate the enemy's camp. There are so many of them against her. We don't know how to get in and the confusion we released is too far from those working on the enemies behalf to help. What can we do?"

The Son shook His head. "First, I'll tell those near her, who love Me to pray more for her. The Holy Spirit will heighten their discernment, patience, strength and desire to fight on her behalf. She has offended and hurt many with her resistance to be introduced to Me so they are weary. While they complete their assignment, find those connected to the people in the enemy's camp who know Us and fight on their behalf. Each person who is being used by the enemy to drag her down has people in their families in relationship with Me. There are more for her and Us than against Us."

The Angels looked perplexed.

The Father nodded.

"The warriors are tired. Can We send in more soldiers? We have been fighting a short time but the battles are intense." The angel lowered his gaze.

The Son looked to the Father.

"It isn't time yet. They are afraid but they will not lose. Tell them to wave My banner over the angels that are weary. We have quite a battle ahead of Us. She'll need all of the warriors later. Patience must have her perfect work. Go back with what the

Son has said and when it's time the strategy will change." The Father said.

"Yes, Lord." The angel retreated.

"Thank you, Father." The Son crumpled in exhaustion. "I know this won't be an easy victory, but she is precious."

"She is precious, like all of My children. We just have to gather the right people around her willing to fight the good fight of faith. Some will introduce You to her, some will show her an example of Your love but she'll come into the knowledge of who We are at her appointed time."

The Son exhaled. "Yes, Lord."

***

One Month Later

Lorraine felt as if an electric current ran through her body. The first two shirts were sweated through before she was out of the front door. She unearthed a set of dress shields her mother sent for her birthday a year ago to use with her third white button down shirt. Any confidence she mustered up over the weekend felt eons away.

Judge Light mastered the look of someone oblivious to the power his black robe yielded over the people sitting in the tables across from him in the picture she scraped up following four hours searching the internet after Tristan went home to his wife and children. A few reporters waited outside of her home as a car service pulled up to take her to the courthouse. She didn't trust herself to drive with her nerves in shambles since the date for her trial was set.

Tristan waited for her inside the doors of the back entrance of the court. Despite her suspension being a judge still had a few privileges. They gathered themselves to walk to the elevator when Tristan placed a halting hand on her forearm. "I'm not sure how you'll feel about it, but I like to pray before I enter court."

"Every time?" Lorraine stared at her lawyer.

Tristan nodded.

"Go for it." Lorraine allowed him to take both of her hands. She was too curious to be embarrassed by an act which she knew looked awkward at best.

Tristan's shoulders eased down. A smile lightened his face as he nodded. "That's better. Let's go win the first day of trial."

***

Day One: Lorraine Allen vs...

"All rise, the honorable Judge Joshua Light presiding." A tall thin African American man entered the courtroom. He took measured steps to the bench before folding into his seat. "You may be seated. We're here to discuss the evidence unearthed in a preliminary hearing against Lorraine Allen regarding unethical practices as an officer of the court."

Everyone in the room was seated. Twelve people waited in the seats to the left of Judge Light. Prosecutor Scribner sat at the table representing the state. A second table filled with people sat behind Scribner.

"Would you like to proceed?" Judge Light nodded toward Prosecutor Scribner. "I want to remind everyone this is a preliminary hearing and you're involvement will determine if further action disciplinary, criminal or civil needs to take place."

"Thank you, Your Honor. We're here today to reveal exculpatory... I mean infallible evidence to show that Judge Lorraine Allen while executing her duties as a trusted officer of the court was engaged in amoral acts with her staff from her bailiff to her clerk. We'll provide witness testimony, communication records and imagery proving the persona of community activist is an act." The Prosecutor tugged the front of the blazer covering a starched stiff white button down shirt into perfect position.

Tristan stood up next to Lorraine. The courtroom appeared lopsided when you considered the number of people on the states side of the court room standing in accusation against Lorraine with only Tristan next to her for defense.

"I want to thank Special Prosecutor Scribner for confidence that the information revealed will be exculpatory in nature since Judge Lorraine Allen has been nothing short of an exemplary citizen and fair officer of the court. We've submitted our request that this preliminary hearing for examination of evidence for formal charging be a bench trial versus jury trial. Due to Judge Allen's position in the community we believe an impartial party is best suited to decide how we proceed, if there is no objection from the prosecution and it pleases the court." Tristan held his breath as he returned to the seat next to Lorraine.

They won't agree to a bench trial for discovery and this mob would bury her under a mountain of every false shred of evidence Scribner and company decided to throw at her. What she hoped would be a quick first day of motions and decisions left the dress shield half soaked through as she watched Judge Light's lips like an addict trying to find a rock in the snow.

"Prosecution has no objection to a bench trial."

Scribner nodded toward Lorraine and Tristan.

"Very well. Jury is dismissed and thanked for your service to the court. We'll be needing to change the schedule of the trial to accommodate the changes. Please meet back here after lunch ready to begin the trial."

Lorraine and Tristan nodded. Scribner made eye contact with Lorraine. No words existed that would do justice to the hatred Lorraine felt growing in her heart for Scribner and company. Two tables of attorneys for an evidentiary trial felt like overkill; it didn't matter to Lorraine. Tristan didn't know and if she had her way, no one would ever know about their circle. She knew she was guilty but so were the people sitting at the table accusing her.

***

Judge Allen's Chambers

Lorraine entered her office. She inhaled the familiar scent of dust, wood polish and fear. With a sigh as she exhaled. When the judge taking over her cases asked to meet with her regarding missing files she raced to the courthouse in record time. Terry walked into the door as Lorraine pulled up a file to email.

"Hey, Your Honor." Terry waited next to Lorraine's desk for instruction.

"Hey, yourself. I wanted to check on you but my lawyer advised that we have as little contact outside of work as possible, you know, due to the allegations of the trial." Lorraine fidgeted in her seat.

Terry nodded.

"The truth about the nature of our relationship will come to the light. I don't expect anyone to accuse you or me about anything after we're cleared. The prosecutor has some kind of vendetta against me." Lorraine shook her head. "I'm rambling. How are you holding up?"

Terry shrugged. "Best as can be expected. As long as this doesn't become a criminal case, I'm good. A condition of my suspended sentence is that I keep my nose clean the balance of my sentence or complete it behind bars."

Lorraine nodded. She was familiar with the details of Terry's freedom. "Keep your head up, consider this a paid vacation for a job well done. I know we'll be exonerated. We have the truth on our side."

"I'd be happier if the truth came with a video of every second we spent together up at your cabin. Someone told me they have pictures of us in compromising positions. I don't even know what that means." Terry said.

"It means they are some low down, dirty conniving liars planting false evidence and Tristan has a great deal of work ahead of him to clear our names." Lorraine pulled several more files and attached them to the folder prepared for transfer to the other Justice.

"So I'm hung out to dry until they decide if they have a case against you." Terry chuckled. "I thought it was crazy in lockdown. People on the outside are worse."

Lorraine shook her head. "You don't belong in that place, Terry. Don't even think that way. This will all blow over."

"Tell that to my kid. Terrance says the treatment from his peers has been craptastic." Terry stood and walked over to a file cabinet next to a floor to ceiling bookcase. "The Nelson case is coming up for review. I'm going to interoffice mail this file so we don't have to come up here again."

"Maybe you should leave it for me to do. This trip up has been the most excitement I've experienced outside of court all week. Scribner is pulling out all the stops and I'm convinced part of the wait is supposed to be some kind of Jedi mind trick to wear us down." Lorraine laughed. "Everyone who knows me is aware that this job is the focal point of my life. My social calendar and work calendar share the same contacts."

Terry placed several files in a neat pile on a secretary in the corner. "Maybe this is a wake up call for you to get a new focal point for your life. You deserve to be happy, Your Honor. It's like you lay it all down for everyone with no regard for yourself."

Lorraine thought about the last party she attended with her inner circle of friends. "That is not true, I enjoy making a difference in other people's lives. That is why I studied law."

"I never met someone who gave it up so freely for so many people." Terry smiled. "You should be getting an award not taken to trial."

"Don't worry about me. I'll put in a few calls to make sure they are keeping a close eye on your boy. Media coverage, peer pressure and bullying are serious. Nothing should be ruining this time for him. You know how important the high school experience is for him, how it impacts who he'll be as a man." Lorraine pulled up her email contact list.

"This is growing him up." Terry nodded.

"You focus on keeping things together and I'll make sure he has an extra set of eyes to keep the craptastic treatment to a minimum." Lorraine gave her clerk a sincere smile. "I'm not anything near perfect but I know they don't have any real evidence because we haven't done anything. This will all blow over."

Terry stood up. "I hope you're right. Terrance gets off the bus in about an hour so I'm gonna send these files off and get home to see how things went today."

"Of course." Lorraine extended her hand. She took Terry's hand in hers. "I know you, Terry. Stop worrying, this will all work out and we'll get back to work in no time."

***

Gentleman's Club

Prosecutor Scribner, Senator Blythe, Judge Carver, Alderman Holt, and Dr. Shields gathered in the back of an exclusive gentleman's club where they paid for a private room and entrance for their circle to gather every other week. Nerves left each of them milling around the table. Senator Blythe and Judge Carver whispered in a corner. Dr. Shields watched Scribner and Senator Blythe go through a file folder at a circular table in the middle of the room.

"Can we get through this so we can get on to some much needed recreation time. The girls are waiting to take all the stress of this matter from us. What do you guys have in that folder?" Judge Carver sat down next to Senator Blythe.

"This is the answer to all our problems." Scribner grinned.

"Spit it out, so we can get on with the rest of the night." Judge Carver reached for the folder.

Scribner snatched it from his reach. "Keep your boxers on, Judge, goodness."

"Don't act like you don't want to get out of yours when the girls get in here as much as I do." Dr. Shields laughed. "Fine, I'll ask like I have some semblance of manners."

"Whatever." Judge Carver shrugged.

"Tell us how those files will solve all of our problems and get this party into gear." Dr. Shields motioned as if he banged a gavel on the table.

"We've spoken with several people who want to retire and get out of the area who'll testify to having less than appropriate propositions from the squeaky clean Lorraine Allen. You know that woman has PAID taxes the last four years. Despite all the people she has access to she hasn't used one questionable tax loophole, all of her investments are safer than peanut butter and jelly. She even volunteers in person at local community centers." Scribner cackled. "If I didn't hate her so much, I'd admire her, but we all know firsthand who she is behind closed doors."

"Yeah, we liked who we knew behind closed doors. You're the only one who had a problem with her. The more I think about it, I'm trying to figure out why our circle has to kick out one of its best people because you don't like her." Dr. Shields crossed his arms.

"Because we agreed that we all had to keep the circle intact. I don't care how much you like what y'all had, she refuses to play ball with everyone and that is a deal breaker. As adventurous as she's been with all of you, she refuses to try something new. That is grounds for dismissal. She doesn't deserve to keep her seat if she didn't earn it." Scribner passed papers to everyone. "You each have connections to the people on the paper I'm giving you. Take time over the next seven days to follow up with them. Find out how far they're willing to go to help mount the case against Lorraine. If we can plant enough in the mind of the jurors--"

"We don't have a jury, Scribner. Her representation dismissed them and you agreed to it smiling like you thought it would work better for us to have no jury. Did you forget the reason for that stupid grin, already?" Senator Blythe smirked.

"No, Walter, I didn't. It is easier to crack one nut than to smooth talk and mesmerize twelve. Don't worry about what is going on in the courtroom, focus on getting some dirt on her with those people or persuading someone to perjure themselves and say she propositioned them. I tried to contact her previous clerk but they aren't able to be found. It's almost like they fell off the face of the earth." Scribner's eyes widened. "Or maybe that is a good thing. I'll get my people to look into what happened to make her last clerk disappear."

"I wish you two could have worked through your differences instead of taking us through all of this drama. Seems a bit extreme. These pictures you have better have them locked in a naked embrace or something or else we could all be screwed." Dr. Shields rubbed his hand over his face.

The lights flickered and a red phone in the corner rang. Senator Blythe made short work of the distance from the table to the phone. Seconds later he returned to the table.

"The girls are worked up and we have some new talent that the manager wants us to break in before he lets them take the stage." Senator Blythe looked at Dr. Shields. "They're known at their old club for taking these things to the next level, looks like Shields has started predicting the future."

"Stop talking in code, Walter." Scribner placed the file in a briefcase.

Senator Blythe smiled. "Boss man, for the club tonight says they're trying to get more girls willing to get down to business quicker and are willing to do for us what Lorraine refused to do for you, Scribner. So let's finish this strategizing and get to what we come here to do."

Alderman Holt, Judge Carver and Dr. Shields laughed. Scribner moved the briefcase to the floor. "You gentleman know I handle business better than all of you with the ladies, so let the games begin."

Chapter 4

ARMY of LITIGATORS

Week Two; Courthouse

Tristan and Lorraine entered the courtroom confident they would be able to put an end to the trial due to the burden of proof on the prosecution. When it came to allegations of moral misconduct of a sexual nature, convictions were uncommon without a smoking gun. No one ever recovered unless it was proven the accuser lied which left many people retired from public service. Lorraine assured Tristan the relationship between her and Terry began and remained professional from their first contact.

Scribner led the army of litigators into the courtroom. They filed into the tables across from Judge Light's bench and the defendants as if they were waiting for the verdict instead of preparing to present the initial evidence. Several people walked into the courtroom behind the prosecution. Lorraine was unable to see because the door to the judge's chamber opened.

"All rise…"

As she stood, Lorraine's mind wandered back to her last get together with the circle at her cabin. Scribner cornered her in the Jacuzzi with a proposition she should have been unable to refuse. Leaving her husband and placing everything on the line to pursue her career aspirations caused her a few sleepless nights. A year in the circle replaced those sleepless nights with advancement and satisfaction she never imagined.

Scribner's request weren't outrageous to some of the other women in the circle but they disgusted Lorraine. No position, connections, not even begging swayed Lorraine's decision. After the first rejection, Scribner only pursued her more. When most people realized the other person wasn't playing hard to get and moved on, Scribner tried harder. Lorraine knew rejection could cause bitterness and resentment but she paid her dues and brought more to the circle than a nice place for their gatherings. Scribner couldn't see past the rejection to admit how valuable Lorraine was to the circle. The others were afraid so now Lorraine would have to make them all see how much they'd miss her since they decided to try to destroy her.

Tristan nudged Lorraine's shoulder for her to take a seat. Her eyes roamed up and down the bailiff's body. She missed her bailiff. The isolation from her job and now the circle left her entire life in disarray.

"We'd like to call our first witness, Vincent White." Scribner looked at Lorraine with lust masked as disgust.

A tall strapping young man she'd had a summer fling with two years ago walked to the front of the courtroom. Lorraine smiled as she relived their innocent encounters. He was foolish enough to believe she wanted to pursue some kind of May-December relationship. Once she satisfied her curiosity and he accompanied her to a few charity events she tried to let him down easy.

"Mr. White, please state your name, age and the nature of your relationship with Lorraine Allen." Scribner stood in front of the state's table.

"I'm Vincent White, thirty one years old and hopelessly in love with Judge Lorraine Allen. We dated briefly twenty eight months ago." Vincent gazed at Lorraine as if she were the only woman in the room.

Tristan turned and looked at his client.

Lorraine dropped her head a bit and blushed. A few wrinkles, a few more inches in places she exercised to keep tight, but she still had it. Her eyes lifted and she gave Vincent a polite nod.

"So you've had sexual relations with a woman who at the time you refer to was appointed to a public office, and more than twenty five years your senior? Care to explain what you received from being part of that ...relationship?" Scribner looked to the judge with a smug nod.

Judge Light gave Scribner a curt nod and turned toward the witness.

"She gave me the most amazing six weeks of my life. We traveled up and down the coast. I accompanied her to several charity functions and met someone who helped me advance my career.

And she isn't twenty five years my senior, I was born twenty eight years too late to sweep her off her feet and love her the way she deserves." Vincent leaned forward in the seat. "I love you, Lorraine. Please give us another chance. If you allow me I promise I'll make you happy."

Scribner took quick steps to the witness. "Mr. White, please just answer the questions. You want this judge to believe that you fell in love with Judge Allen, a woman old enough to be your mother, grandmother in some cases. How much money, how many favors... What did it cost her to buy this love and devotion from you?"

Lorraine suppressed a laugh.

Tristan leaned over and whispered. "Judge Allen, is there anything about your relationship with Mr. White you need to tell me."

Lorraine attempted to wipe the smile from her face. "No. We shared an innocent romance. I didn't even pay for anything when we went out. He insisted on paying for everything, even the chewing gum."

Tristan nodded.

"It didn't cost her anything to be herself. The only favor she did for me was to spend her time away from the court and her charity work with me." Vincent stared with love and affection at Lorraine. "She is the sexiest woman I know. Her age doesn't matter; I'd marry her tomorrow if she'd have me."

"No further questions for the defendant." Scribner stormed back to the table.

"Your witness, Mr. Reeves." Judge Light said.

"Mr. White, during your time with Judge Allen, is it true you paid for everything when you went out in public?" Tristan stood behind the table next to Lorraine.

"Of course. I'm young but I'm a man. No woman of Lorraine's caliber should be expected to pay for anything while she is out with me. I remember getting upset when we stopped at a small gas station one weekend riding up the coast when she tried to pay for chewing gum. It insulted me. I'm well versed in how to treat a lady. You pull out chairs, open doors and give them preference. Not because their weak, because their worth that and more." Vincent said.

"I have no further questions, your Honor." Tristan sat in his seat.

"Redirect your Honor." Scribner shot up from the prosecution's table.

Judge Light nodded.

"Judge Allen seems to have made quite an impression on you, did this happen before or after you shared a bed with her?" Scribner stared at Lorraine.

"Objection, your honor." Tristan rose. "There is no moral clause in Judge Allen's contract that stops her from having a consensual relationship with this or anyone else."

"Sustained. Prosecution allegations state that Judge Allen used her power and position to force or manipulate people into inappropriate relationships." Judge Light cleared his throat.

"Yes, your Honor." Scribner sighed. "No further questions for this witness."

"Mr. White, please take your seat." Judge Light said. "Prosecutor."

"I'd like to call former classmate of Terry Johnson," Scribner turned toward the people in the seats behind the defendants and prosecution.

Tristan leaned toward Lorraine. "Do you know, Sidney Smead?"

Lorraine shook her head. "I know an Anthony Smead."

Tristan sat upright.

"Sidney please tell the court the details of your relationship with Judge Allen.

Sidney looked into Lorraine's eyes with hate. Lorraine thought Sidney looked familiar but didn't remember how or why she knew the witness. "Yes, we had an affair the summer I cleaned her office as part of work release from the prison. Johnson told me about this judge who helped prisoners get out with special circumstances so I wrote and asked for a chance to work under the work release program. For six months every time she was in her office when I cleaned it, she forced me to have sex with her. When she realized I wasn't available enough she came on to my brother, Anthony, who transported me on the days I was allowed to visit our sick mother in the hospital. It was disgusting the things she made me do with her. I'm ashamed but I had to come forward when I found out she was doing the same thing to Terry."

Lorraine gasped. She fought the urge to stand up and call Sidney a lying waste of skin.

Tristan broke into a sweat. "Lorraine." He whispered.

"It's a lie, Tristan, I swear. Anthony didn't respond well when I ended our relationship. From what I hear, he left town after and hasn't been back since. This is revenge. I didn't do any of those things." Lorraine said through clenched teeth.

"No further questions, your Honor." Scribner smiled.

"Defense requests the right to call the witness back at a later time." Tristan said.

"Granted. Please step down." Judge Light nodded at the witness.

"We need to talk, Lorraine. I feel like there is something you're not telling me." Tristan whispered.

Lorraine nodded. The air in the room felt too thick to speak. She feared she may scream and be unable to stop. Things weren't going to be cleared up as easy as she thought if Scribner was bringing in people to lie. Her only way to discredit the testimony of Sidney Smead and two others who repeated similar stories was to find Anthony and convince him to come home and testify on her behalf.

***

Home of Terry Johnson

Terry walked into the house hoping to get a few minutes of solitude and quiet before Terrance walked in from school. The key turned in the door. The aroma of pastry beckoned from the table. Voices carried into the foyer from the living room. "Hello. Mom is that you?"

Silence meant trouble. Terry remembered that from lockdown.

Someone cleared their throat.

"Who's there?"

A shadow moved in the living room.

Terry took cautious steps toward the shadow. "Terrance?"

"What happened to you?" Terry rushed to get a closer look at the boy's face.

"There was a little problem at school, but I took care of it." Terrance raised a self-conscious hand to his swollen right eye. "Those guys won't mess with me again. They were saying nasty mean things about you."

"And that gave you a reason to put your hands on them? No." Terry's breathing became hurried.

"You don't have to deal with them everyday. You don't hear the things they say about you, behind my back or to my face. I got tired of it and I did something about it. When you were in prison you said people tested you all the time and you had to defend yourself. So did I." Terrance's chest swelled with anger.

"Good grief, you act just like your mother sometimes." Terry chuckled and hugged him. "Get some more ice on that eye and let me see the paper they sent home from school."

Terrance smirked. "They didn't send anything, no one saw the fight. It happened in the boy's locker room between classes."

Terry pondered the situation and thought about all of the things that could've happened if someone had discovered them fighting in the locker room. No matter how much help the Judge offered, the thought of leaving Terrance in school during the scandal left too many opportunities for him to start down the wrong path. "I'm going down to your school to speak with someone."

"C'mon, it's not that serious. You should see what the other guy looks like." Terrance laughed.

"I'm gonna bring you home from school until all of this blows over. You need to focus on your studies and not be distracted with what some stupid kids are saying. Don't worry about anything. I'll take care of it." Terry said.

"Thanks." Terrance gave Terry a hug.

"No problem. That is what I'm supposed to do. You're my number one priority." Terry said.

"You didn't do what they said with Judge Allen, did you? She seems like a nice lady and I saw her looking at that bailiff's butt. She never looked twice at you." Terrance stared into Terry's eyes.

Terry placed one hand on each side of Terrance's shoulders. "Prison doesn't rob you of your morals and standards unless you let it. Nothing is going on between Judge Allen and me except for work."

Terrance nodded.

"I'll be back." Terry walked out of the door.

***

Terry walked into the office hoping to find an administrator, at least a guidance counselor or a secretary to make an appointment. Someone needed to help remove Terrance from his classes until everything with the trial blew over. A bell rang. Terry jumped. Loud noises are less welcome than silence when you've been locked up.

A woman walked into a door under a sign that said main office. Terry followed.

"Good afternoon. We'll be with you in a moment." The secretary turned her attention to Terry. "If you don't have an appointment please sign in with what you need."

Terry nodded, affixed a post-it note and wrote on the clipboard under the woman who entered the office. Moments felt like hours. The secretary motioned for the woman to follow her to a door marked, "guidance." Another woman walked in with a couple of boys wearing the standard issue saggy skinny jeans and skateboard style checkered shirt. The new style baffled Terry.

"Johnson?" The secretary called. "I can't understand the first name."

"Terry Johnson." Terry joined the woman at the counter.

"I read your post-it note and the principal has agreed to speak with you." The secretary motioned for Terry to follow down a corridor. The hallway led to a door. A younger man than Terry expected opened the door to a modest space. Plaques and framed diplomas offered the most distinguished touches to the decor.

"Ms. Snow gave me the post it note and I'm aware of the hard time the other kids are giving Terrance. How can I help you?" The principal sat in the aged chair. A worn name plate reflected a glint of light from the sun through the window.

"Principal Harris, I'm concerned about the altercation that bruised Terrance's eye. He and some other boys fought in the locker room. No one caught them. I don't want this on his permanent record in light of the reason his behavior has changed." Terry averted the principal's eyes. "If you watch the news you know what is happening with my boss. I'd like to take him out of school and guide him through his course work the rest of the semester or year. Once I'm exonerated he'll return to school."

Principal Harris nodded. "I'll have to speak to his teachers but that shouldn't be a problem in light of the circumstances. You're sure you want to do this?"

Terry's head dropped. It lifted with a nod. "I'll bring him for tests, if you prefer, as long as their scheduled when he won't have to interact with the boys he fought. Keeping him on the right track is my priority. It is not the school's responsibility to protect him."

"We don't want anything to happen to Terrance either. I understand your concern. I'll contact you with the details myself." Principal Harris said.

"Thank you." Terry leaned forward to stand.

"I remember you from school, and I know what you did for your brother landed you in prison. No one believes you did what they say you did with Judge Allen." Principal Harris said. "We're here to help you in whatever way we can."

Terry smiled. "I appreciate that. Talk to you soon."

***

Lorraine Allen's Home

Lorraine sat in the garage in her car for an hour after she returned home from the courthouse. Silence felt so cold and sterile she hated the thought of being there, in her home, alone until the next morning. Tristan talked with her about the other inmates who testified against her. She couldn't believe they found people willing to lie, under oath about her and Terry. No one knew about her private life, but most people knew Terry wasn't capable of the allegations. Everyone knew Terry went to jail on a bum rap to allow that good for nothing older brother to go to college on scholarship. No one felt worse for Terry than Lorraine when that same brother died in a car accident months before graduation.

Terry's fortitude in the face of tragedy escaped Lorraine. She didn't understand how someone could face so much negativity and still be positive. Gurgling sounds from her stomach forced Lorraine to leave the garage. Her kitchen hadn't been stocked with so much food since she asked her husband to move out. Most meals happened in restaurants and special parties with her old circle. Anger coursed through her body as she thought of their betrayal.

The doorbell rang.

Lorraine smiled. Her feet carried her to the door. The smile melted away.

Rachel waved.

Lorraine opened the door. "Hey, sis."

Rachel pulled Lorraine into a long hug.

Lorraine closed her eyes and reveled in the comfort of her sister's arms. A sound behind Rachel pulled her from the solace. "Hey, Barry."

Rachel rubbed Lorraine's back. "We can stay out here but I'm sure that we'd be more comfortable inside. Barry brought your favorite Chinese takeout."

Barry lifted a bag into Lorraine's view.

A smile covered Lorraine's face. She led them into the dining room.

"Thanks." Barry walked around Lorraine and placed the bag on the table. He exited toward the kitchen and returned with wine and glasses. "I figured soda wouldn't be strong enough. It's been a wine kinda week."

Rachel gave Lorraine a nervous half smile.

Lorraine shook her head.

Barry shrugged. He pulled containers from the plastic encased brown paper bag, a container and plastic bowl with lid was placed in front of Lorraine's normal seat and a Styrofoam container in front of Barry and next to him.

Rachel sat in the chair next to Barry.

Lorraine took her seat.

Rachel and Barry held hands with bowed heads.

Barry bowed his head. "Lord, bless this food. In Jesus' name. Amen."

"Amen." Rachel said.

Lorraine raised the fork to her mouth. "Yep."

Barry gave Rachel a side look.

Rachel studied her chicken fried rice. "So, how you holding up?"

"Better than I could." Lorraine lifted a spoonful of egg drop soup to her lips.

"How are your connections?" Rachel poked her plastic fork around in the veggie fried rice.

"What do you need, Rachel?" Lorraine placed her spoon next to the takeout container.

"It's not Rachel, it's me." Barry looked Lorraine in the eyes. "There have been unexpected repercussions from your situation."

Lorraine stared at her sister with one eyebrow raised.

"What Barry is trying to say is that his business has seen a drastic drop in clientele since this whole mess with you went to trial. He was able to stave off the questions and speculations but when you weren't absolved from a preliminary hearing people started boycotting him." Rachel sniffed.

Lorraine fought an urge to roll her eyes. Rachel's melodramatic antics, crocodile tears and innocent brown eyes landed her in more predicaments during high school than she cared to recall.

Barry rubbed his wife's back.

"We know how well connected you are to some very important people." Rachel blinked back tears.

"Lorraine, we know this is a lot to ask but do you think you could at least think about it."

Rachel sighed.

Lorraine wanted to tell them about those important people. A desire to unburden her soul and tell them about all the favors she'd already exchanged with those important people. She needed to tell someone the truth about those important people.

Rachel stared into Lorraine's eyes.

Barry took his wife's hand.

"Are you serious? I'm supposed to take a moment from fighting to clear my name to call in a favor with the people bringing false charges up against me. You two have lost more than a few clients." Lorraine laughed. "You might want to learn how to ask God to do more than bless your food, because that would take a miracle."

Chapter 5

PICTURES

Week Three; Courthouse

Tristan walked back and forth in the hallway before the entrance to the court. Lorraine drank him in from head to toe because she felt uncomfortable lusting after him in close proximity. She wasn't sure if it was the unfamiliar love that resonated in his voice when he talked about his wife and their children, but she didn't like the feeling. After one last glance she smiled and interrupted his pace.

"Good morning, Tristan, you look like you're about to burst at the seams." Lorraine said.

"Good morning, Judge Allen. There is something we missed at the beginning of the trial and I've been unable to put my finger on it but I'm sure if I just listen close enough it will come to me." Tristan nodded and stepped around her to continue pacing.

Prosecutor Scribner approached Lorraine as Tristan shifted his march further down the hall to give her room at the intersection of the two corridors. Disgust welled up in Lorraine so much she had to lean on the wall to steady herself.

"You know this could all be avoided with a discreet trip up to the cabin." Scribner flashed a magnetic smile.

"Go straight to hell." Lorraine flashed an even bigger smile. "You are risking a lot for a few moments that may not be worth everything you're risking to get me removed from a seat I earned."

"Laying on your back doesn't earn you anything, unless you're doing it with the right people." Scribner invaded Lorraine's personal space. "You're risking a lot for something you might discover you'll enjoy, or is that what you're afraid of?"

"Who said I don't know whether I'd enjoy it or not. You're assuming too much about me, which is one of the reasons I never wanted to be with you. You don't know how to listen. Lousy listeners tend to be lousy lovers." Lorraine stepped back and smiled again. "Good day, Counselor. I'll see you in court."

Scribner fumed as Lorraine and Tristan walked past her into the courtroom. Defense and prosecution assembled in their prospective areas. A large projector was set up to the left of the prosecution's side of the court. The bailiff walked in and Judge Light entered in his customary fashion.

"Please be seated." Judge Light cleared his throat. "Good morning, everyone. Prosecutor Scribner, please proceed."

"Thank you. I've received some photographs and wanted to present them as evidence today and some correspondence between Judge Allen and several of the witnesses about the abuse of power exacted by Judge Allen to force them to succumb to her demands." Scribner strolled over to the projector.

Tristan rocked back and forth in his seat like his bladder would burst. The air in the room felt heavy. Scribner powered on all of the equipment then returned to the table for the prosecution.

"The first set of pictures will show several shots of Judge Allen in a compromising position with our second witness Sidney Smead. The shots display Judge Allen with Sidney in a less consensual position." Scribner looked toward Judge Allen's table.

Lorraine squinted at the picture. She recognized the shot, she recognized Sidney five years younger at a party she attended with Sidney's brother. Their clothes and body positioning looked awkward. Tristan nudged Lorraine's arm.

"Do you see something odd about the picture? You look perturbed." Tristan said.

Lorraine nodded. She couldn't put her finger on it but something was not right with the photo although she did remember being at the event with Anthony.

Tristan cleared his throat. He stood.

The court fell hush.

Judge Light shifted his attention from the screen to Tristan.

"Mr. Reeves is there something you need?" Judge Light said.

"I've been studying Judge Allen's contract of service. There is a step in her investigative period that was not completed by the ethics board that requested this inquisition into her conduct. Without any of that work done, this hearing isn't supposed to happen." Tristan paused and picked up a copy of the contract. "May I approach?"

Judge Light nodded.

Tristan walked to the bench. He handed a stack of papers with tabs affixed to several areas and what looked like a large highlighted area. Judge Light accepted the papers from the Tristan. Lorraine held her breath.

Silence filled every crevice of the courtroom.

Judge Light looked over the information then back to Scribner's table. "In light of the stipulations of the contract we must wait and complete a thorough investigation based on the criteria. If they are not satisfied all of the allegations must be dropped and Judge Allen reinstated."

Scribner swayed next to the projector.

"Court is adjourned until the investigation is completed." Judge Light banged his gavel.

***

Lorraine walked out of the courtroom in shock. She blinked. She pinched herself. A red mark stared at her from her forearm. In her haste to convince the rational people in her circle not to allow Scribner to destroy her she'd overlooked law school 101, make sure the opponent follows all the rules. Murderers walked free on technicalities too much for her to think it didn't work. A whistle crossed her lips as she exited the courthouse.

"Judge Allen." Tristan called out behind her. He ran to catch up to her less than ten feet from her house.

"Tristan," Lorraine forced herself to calm her raging hormones. The only thing more attractive than a firm body was an intelligent mind. "Bravo, you delivered an amazing performance today."

Tristan blushed.

The uncomfortable feeling she hated, returned. "How did you find that clause buried in all of that minutiae?"

"It was on my to-do list once I looked over the evidentiary report from Prosecutor Scribner. When they pushed the date of the trial up I was forced to abandon my initial schedule. The expedited date didn't allow me to look over it in detail until this weekend."

"Genius." Lorraine shook her head. She knew Judge Carver was the brains behind pulling the strings responsible for pushing her court date up. Tristan's smile pulled Lorraine from her thoughts. "You're an excellent lawyer, Tristan."

"That means a lot coming from you, Judge Allen." Tristan beamed with pride. The light emitted from Tristan's smile faded. "There is one small problem with this discovery and the recess of court proceedings. The conditions of your contract call for all evidence and charges be brought to evidence together so an investigation of your life is going to ensue. In addition to them being able to prove the current allegations they're going to dig through your finances, your community service, your entire life is under their legal investigative discretion."

Lorraine smiled so hard her cheeks ached. "That is fine. The only thing they could try to accuse me of is not having a normal social life. My business and personal address share all the same names. No one is going to be able to accuse me of missing a dot on an 'I' because my work is ninety percent of my life."

"That is great. I knew you weren't guilty." Tristan nodded. He grinned again. His smile wavered. "What about the other ten percent?"

"Judge Light made it clear, when Scribner attempted to paint my menopause driven stamina as a crime that the only activity open for discussion would be things that people have done as a result of abusing my power." Lorraine resisted the urge to proposition Tristan to celebrate the temporary interruption to her witch hunt. "I assure you, Tristan, you, nor them can find anyone who did anything with me against their will. Willingness is in my top three on my list of attractive traits in a man, right after a hard body and intelligence."

Tristan cleared his throat. "Well, I believe you. Let's see what happens when they summon us back to court."

***

Three Days Later

Scribner slammed papers down and chucked the file cabinet holding closed case files on to the ground. Judge Carver and Senator Blythe entered the room. They looked at each other with slight concern.

"I take it she hasn't offered up the resignation you boasted we'd get while you were enjoying your lap dance at the club last week." Senator Blythe stepped over the cabinet.

"This is the worst time for your corny jokes and unwitting one liners, Walter." Scribner stomped so hard the desk shook. "How does she keep getting so close to being defeated only to be pulled from the fire? I'm pissed, her and that snot nosed junior attorney made me feel like a fool."

Judge Carver released a throaty laugh. It bounced around the office as Senator Blythe and Scribner froze. "You sure that isn't sexual frustration? I saw the two of you outside of the courtroom while that junior attorney marched up and down the corridor mumbling to himself. I've never seen a woman more aroused or arousing."

"She prefers young chippies. From what I hear, her young esquire is a bible thumper of the most devoted kind. With no access to the circle and an impenetrable fortress around that young man she is probably running through batteries or climbing up the walls." Scribner laughed.

"We should drop this and find you someone new to play with because you're going to lose this battle. I'm not willing to lose everything I've worked to achieve because you couldn't get your itch for Lorraine scratched. Find a younger, firmer version of her and satisfy that perverted appetite of yours." Senator Blythe said.

"You underestimate me, sir. I believe I'll have my cake and ice cream too. No one rejects me and gets away with it, not without limping away." Scribner plopped down in the Italian leather executive chair behind the mahogany antique desk to match the turned over file cabinet.

"That is where you're wrong, counselor. I'm well aware of your reach and prowess. I just believe you've finally met your match but she won't cooperate. The question is does that anger or attract you. We aren't willing to lose our lives while you find out. Judge Light looked pissed about the lack of proper investigation. You have that little crew of dirt diggers pull out the heavy duty excavation equipment, you need to unearth something buried deep enough to make her fall into the hole and disappear forever. I've known Lorraine longer than I've known you, hell has no fury like that woman scorned."

Scribner's smile disappeared. "Please, don't insult me. The devil takes his torture technique lessons from me."

***

Eternity: Throne of Grace

The angels kneeled before the Father and the Son. Wings tattered and dingy, the one on the left took several moments to stand. The one the right remained on one knee.

"Master, the battle is going better but the humans are afraid to share Your gospel. There is a barrier around her. She is present but inaccessible. Her heart is open to give but closed to receive. She gives to relieve the pressure of being so isolated within herself. The need for You is there but she doesn't know how to express it or accept it and the people are afraid to speak to her about You." The standing angel kneeled.

The kneeling angel stood. "We've had small victories but Tristan, Rachel and Mrs. Johnson are becoming battle fatigued."

The Son looked at the Father. A hush settled over the heavens. The cries of the saints came up before the Father. Another sound in the distance of souls tormented by hell fire attempted to push through the heavenly realm past the prayers and worship of the Father's children. The sound of Lorraine's ex husband's voice and his new wife crying out Lorraine's name touched both the Father and the Son's heart.

"There is great turmoil and the battlefield of Lorraine's mind has been under the enemy's control for many years. Don't allow her demeanor to distract You as You monitor the battlefield and send the warrior angels of the people We've sent to lead her to know Our love into the fight. The enemy is determined to keep her soul but We will prevail. She is chosen. My Son died for her, My desire is for everyone to come into a full relationship with Us. Don't let those close to her grow weary in their part of the battle. You have My word and it always accomplishes what I send it to do. Continue to fight on to lighten the burden for Lorraine, Tristan and his wife, Dyson, and Mrs. Johnson. We will not lose this battle." The Father looked at the Son.

"Thank You, Father. The Holy Spirit will be notified to strengthen and comfort those in the middle of the battle. They are not going to lose. We have already provided everything they need to win inside of them in the Holy Spirit. This battle looks worse than it is." The Son waved the angel's dismissal.

The angels bowed and exited the throne room.

"You are determined to save this woman's soul." The Father said.

"It is the reason You sent Me there, You're desire was for all to be in relationship with Us." The Son shook his head. "She doesn't realize she needs Us but she'll know when this is all over. I've already set up everything needed to break through the barriers around her heart."

"I love her enough to send You, of course I want her to know Us, but she has to choose it for herself. We won't compromise Our principles." The Father turned toward the Son.

"Her will won't be violated, but the circumstances are perfect to make her willing to enter into a relationship with Us because it is what she chooses." The Son smiled. "You know the end."

"I knew it from her beginning." The Father said.

Chapter 6

THE MOB

One Month Later; Courthouse

Lorraine sat on a bench across from the courtroom. Tristan sounded hopeful when he brought a copy of the report from the investigation. She laughed as the truth about her stared up at her in black and white. The remainder of the trial would be centered on allegations she did not hold up the ethical expectations of the people.

"Good morning, Judge Allen." Scribner smirked.

Lorraine rolled her eyes.

"Tell your counsel thank you for the additional time to mount a better case against you." Scribner said.

Lorraine stood. "Go to hell."

"We'll share a pilot light." Scribner laughed and entered the courtroom followed by the legal team.

Tristan approached Lorraine. "Everything is gonna work out, Lorraine. Don't look so worried. I prayed and I have it on good authority God is going to restore you."

Lorraine stared at Tristan.

"Let's go inside." Tristan opened the door for her.

***

Tristan held the door open for Lorraine as they exited the court.

"I'm going to resign from my seat, sell my house and move to another state to practice law. This has gone too far." Lorraine said as they walked to the elevator.

"That is not necessary. Remember what I told you this morning. God is going to work this out. The prosecution thinks this proves they were right but it doesn't, their lack of willingness to follow proper procedure shows they are not to be trusted. Judge Light isn't fooled by the circumstantial evidence they've presented so far."

Lorraine and Tristan entered the elevator. "I hope you're right. I'm not perfect, Tristan. Despite the squeaky clean nature of the investigation there are things in my personal life many people wouldn't approve of if brought before the public."

"Anything that can help me prepare for the coming information will only help me defend you better, Lorraine." Tristan pressed the lobby button.

Lorraine nodded.

***

Same Day: Terry Johnson's Home

A knock on the door startled Mrs. Johnson. She made quick steps to the front door. The middle of a chest blocked the view in her peephole.

"Who is it?" Mrs. Johnson said.

"I'm looking for Terry Johnson." The chest boomed.

Terry walked up to the door. "What is going on?"

"One moment." Mrs. Johnson looked at Terry. "Look through the peephole. Now you tell me what is going on?"

Terry mimicked Mrs. Johnson. "I don't know that chest."

"Who's at the door?" Terrance walked up behind them.

"Go back and finish studying, Terrance." Mrs. Johnson said.

Terrance shrugged and left the foyer.

Terry opened the door. "Can I help you?"

A massive hand shoved a file folder in front of Terry's face. "This is a request from Special Prosecutor Scribner asking you to work with us to indict Judge Allen and expose your relationship."

Terry refused to take the folder.

Mrs. Johnson plucked the papers from the man's large hand. "Thank you, sir. Terry will look over the information and get back with someone. I assume there is contact information in here somewhere."

He nodded. His back seemed more massive than his chest. A chill ran through Terry's body.

Mrs. Johnson closed the front door.

Terrance cleared his throat. "He looked like someone from the mob. My goodness he had to be almost seven feet tall."

Terry shrugged. "Doesn't matter, I'm not lying like I heard those other people did for this Scribner. Judge Allen has been good to me, to this family. I'm not going to bail on her."

"Humph." Mrs. Johnson walked into the kitchen

"What is that supposed to mean, Mother?" Terry followed.

"She hasn't talked to you since you met her in the office to turn the case files over to the other judge. Don't go down with a sinking ship. If she isn't guilty she has pissed someone very powerful off. Ruining you and sending you back to prison is collateral damage. They aren't interested in ruining you... Help them get her and keep your job in the process." Mrs. Johnson turned her back and started a tea kettle.

"You can't be serious." Terry plopped down in the chair across from Terrance. "She hasn't done anything to deserve that, she has been a good boss, mentor and friend."

"No one cares about the truth, Terry. This is your life, your freedom on the line. Terrance is being harassed so much he has to be home schooled and you won't be on paid leave forever. Take care of you. You don't have a fancy law degree to fall back on."

"What do you think, Terrance?" Terry said.

"Makes good sense. I don't want you to go back to prison and I want to go back to school." Terrance shrugged. "On the other hand you said honesty is the best policy. I don't know what you should do, but I hope this is all over soon."

Terry looked at Terrance, Mrs. Johnson and sighed.

***

Same Day; Lorraine's House

Lorraine unlocked the door and returned to the living room. Her brother-in-law and sister followed. She took a seat on the sofa.

"You look better, Lorraine." Rachel smiled as she sat next to Barry on the loveseat.

"So do you, I assume business has picked back up." Lorraine settled under a handmade throw.

"Yep. I don't know who you called but I'm glad you did. Some of the people are just curious about doing business with someone connected to someone involved in a scandal." Barry laughed and rubbed his hands together.

"Glad to know my misfortune is helping someone." Lorraine said.

Rachel shot her husband a look of disdain. "Barry, doesn't mean to be insensitive, Lorraine. You know how stressed he was before they paused the trial. Now that they have decided to continue it is easier for people to be comfortable asking more detailed questions. I have talked to many people who don't believe it because the rest of your life is so dull."

"A girl's gotta have some fun." Lorraine wiggled her eyebrows.

Rachel gasped.

Barry laughed.

"Relax little sister. I'm not having a forced affair with Terry, I'm not an ogre. Forcing people to be with me is the last thing I have to do." Lorraine shook her head.

Barry stood. "I'm famished. Gonna go pick up something for us to munch on."

Rachel nodded.

Barry pecked her on the left temple.

Rachel scooted herself to sit next to Lorraine on the couch. She touched her sister's blanketed foot. "You can drop the brave front. What is really going on with you, Lorraine?"

Lorraine gave her sister a confused look.

"I know how much you sacrificed to pursue your career. Dyson is remarried with children. Kenya told me she only sees you two or three times a year. Who only sees their best friend two or three times a year? I'd see you less than that if it weren't for the holiday get togethers you show up to out of obligation." Rachel took the second throw from the back of the sofa and draped it over her legs. "You made your career your life and now they're trying to take it from you. I want to know how you're doing."

Lorraine stared at the pattern on Rachel's blanket.

Rachel leaned forward and waved her hand in front of Lorraine's face. "Talk to me. If you don't let some of that off your chest you're going to explode."

"I probably will. My normal outlet for letting off steam has been blocked." Lorraine chuckled. She ran a tired hand over her face. Tears crept to the edge of her eyes. "If you must know, little sister, things could be better. My job...My career is my life. I'm terrified."

Chapter 7

CONFESSION

Eternity: Throne of Grace

"The Judge has not confessed her sins. She won't do it. Give me access to her body. If you allow me to make her ill, she'll die and I can have what is mine. I want what's mine, her soul." Satan hissed every "s."

"No." The Father said.

"She misses fornicating with Senator Blythe, Judge Carver, Alderman Holt, Dr. Shields and Mark Jones. Misses it because she is evil. You're not her Father, I am. Every time she opens her mouth to Tristan, she lies. Refuses to tell him the truth about what kind of person she is behind closed doors. Stop protecting her, she doesn't need or want Your love. I'll never allow her to know it is here for her. Your Son knows how much her body craves satiation. Give me her soul. Let me put her out of her misery." Satan said.

"Your words are true." The Father sighed. He looked to Earth. Tristan's head bowed over his desk. A prayer for Lorraine lifted to heaven.

Satan scowled.

"You have legal grounds to continue to take everything from her but you're not to touch her health. The prayers of those who love My Son and I surround her. If you find a place where they have not covered her you are within your rights to attack her there but do not touch her with an illness." The Father said.

The Son frowned.

Satan smiled.

"Father, let me stand in for her. I beg of You, I plead with You to let me hear the things the imps, demons and spirits are saying to keep her from hearing the words of those We've assigned to share Our love with her. Don't look at her based on her actions, see her through My blood, that is Mrs. Johnson's prayer daily. Hear her prayer Father, she desires Terry and Lorraine to come to know You as a result of this trial. Please hear her request."

"As You request, Son. That prayer will bring forth My will. Continue to assign intercessors who want to see My will done in their lives and We'll continue to make advances. The church where Mrs. Johnson attends is full of ignorance based witchcraft. Their prayers blocked hers while she was there, I'm glad she began praying at home. They believe praying what they want outside of My will is helping, tell the Holy Spirit to teach them praying outside of My plan and will, knowing or unknowingly for what they believe are good reasons is witchcraft." The Father looked at the enemy.

Satan glared at the Son.

The Son smiled. "Thank You, Father. I will, they thought they were helping but they were deceived by the enemy. He sent false prophets and teachers to lead them away from a posture of love and compassion when praying. Please forgive them."

"Consider it forgotten." The Father and Son turned to look at the enemy.

"This isn't over." Satan mumbled.

"Your business is done, LEAVE!" The Son pointed in the direction the enemy entered. "Leave the way you came."

***

"Tonight on the 6 o'clock news we have a ground breaking investigation into the seedy side of political aspirations. Where lust, desire and lies pave the way to high profile positions. Scott has our story. Scott?" The voice faded as the introduction music for the six o'clock news hour faded.

"Inside sources have leaked damning information that may explain the accelerated rise of legal phenomenon and community service star Judge Lorraine Allen. It has come to the attention of the Channel 3 News that Judge Allen and several other prominent community and political figures have exchanged back-room deals for bedroom deals to advance each other's careers for years." Scott turned his head to a different camera. "This Circle has been in existence for years. We will bring you exclusive knowledge of its existence with more details to come tonight on the 9 o'clock news."

Pictures flashed on the screen of several of the prisoners paid to testify on behalf of the prosecutor. Several of them looked content and one looked petrified. Two of the pictures were taken outside of the same bank. Scott looked at the forward facing camera with his eyebrow raised.

"Disgusting and demoralizing conduct of this nature is expected by the dregs of society. No one wants to believe the public officers we pay to live just, upstanding lives would be so lewd in their private affairs or use the intimate moments of their lives for professional or political gains."

Scott whipped his head to a different camera on the opposite side of the room from the first shift. "It does make you question the validity of the testimony from the character witnesses presented by the prosecution. If Judge Allen's needs being met for personal and professional advancement, why force almost paroled prisoners to participate in unsavory relations?"

***

Senator Blythe's House

Scribner rushed through Senator Blythe's front door. The atmosphere reeked of fear and anger. Judge Carver, Dr. Shields, Alderman Holt and several others waited in the library. Senator Blythe greeted Scribner with a nod toward the chair at the head of his meeting table.

"Don't be shy now, Scribner, you've been steering this boat the whole time. Come take the helm." Dr. Shields crossed his arms.

Fresh manicured hands smoothed a brand new Armani suit as Scribner took purposed steps to the front of the table. "Now ladies, let's not get our panties in a bunch."

"You know every man in this room well enough to know… We don't wear women's panties." Alderman Holt said.

"If we did, it would only be because you liked it, Scribner." Judge Carver sneered at Scribner.

"Enough." Senator Blythe stood next to Scribner at the head of the table. "No one forced anyone to become part of the circle. Each and every one of you were recommended or applied for membership after a vigorous investigation into your connections and motives. We all knew the risks were high and decided to take them. Now is not the time to attack each other."

"Thank you, Senator." Scribner said. "This leak is not something we have to run and hide from. If we respond to the allegations properly it is possible we can use the news media to convict Judge Allen and have her removed without finishing the trial."

Judge Carver leaned forward. "You've lost your mind. This is bigger than Lorraine not meeting your freaky sneaky sex demands. It is possible for people not to be into your brand of freakiness. No matter how irresistible you believe yourself to be, it happens. Get over it and stop this craziness before we're all exposed."

Murmurs and grumbling filled the space around the table.

Scribner's head dropped. "So you think I can just walk into the courtroom tomorrow and end this. What do you propose I do say...oops, never mind. We're in too deep. No one is going to go for that with all the attention this story has brought. Kicking her off the bench may be the sacrifice people are hungry for now."

"Kicking her off the bench is the revenge you've been hungry for since she rejected your tired pick up lines. I'll tell you one thing, Scribner, if this doesn't work or I'm exposed. Yours will be the first behind hung out to dry with mine." Judge Carver crossed his arms.

Scribner sighed. "Is there anyone else who agrees with the good judge?"

Several hands shot into the air, half of the people wanted the witch hunt to be abandoned.

"How many people trust me to take care of this without the need to abandon the circle?"

The other half of the people's hands shot up.

Everyone raised their hand except for one person. Scribner turned to him.

"Congressman, you've failed to vote either way. That may be allowed on Capitol Hill but we need to know where you stand." Scribner said.

"I'm standing right here. You're plan doesn't need my vote, no matter what you think should happen the people voted me into office. I'm not guilty of anything other than having a healthy sex drive. You'll have to find someone else for your tie breaker." Senator Blythe said.

***

Same Day; Lorraine's Home

Lorraine nestled up next to Nelson. The screen on the television flickered and switched to the Channel 3 9 o'clock news. Nelson reached to turn the station but Lorraine placed her hand on his arm.

Pictures of Lorraine, witnesses who testified at the hearing and stock images of question marks filled her screen. Lorraine leaned forward. "Now what?"

"Scott Lovitt, reporting with breaking developments about the high brow sex bartering society which may be responsible for the rise of several community leaders including Lorraine Allen. We have received pictures of several members of this group at a holiday mixer at the judge's vacation cabin." Scott nodded and the screen changed to a new screen showing photos at the same cabin being passed off as her cabin in the courtroom video.

The air in the room became dense. Nelson peeled Lorraine from his side. He looked at her as if horns grew from her scalp. She ignored him. A lightning bolt hit her. Every decision and deal she made to advance her career floated around in her mind.

Visions of Dyson moving out flashed before her eyes. Memories of invitations to events with Kenya, her sister and others she once shared a serious bond with floated through her mind. No one knew how much she sacrificed to leave a legacy and now careless actions by someone upset she was not willing to abandon the final shred of her morals wanted to erase every good thing she'd done.

Lorraine's head shook. "This is not happening. Why are they trying to destroy me?"

Nelson pulled her back into his chest and allowed her to cry.

Ten minutes later Lorraine dried her eyes with the sheet from her bed.

"I knew it couldn't be true. You're too good a person to be part of something that reckless and seedy. You're in better shape than most women half your age. I've seen how you give fair judgment and mentor the less fortunate." Nelson rubbed his warm hand across her bare skin.

"I'm not perfect, Nelson. We've been doing this for years, you're my co-worker… We shouldn't be doing this either." Lorraine shook her head.

"This is consensual. I pursued you." Nelson kissed her bare shoulder. "There is nothing seedy and reckless about what we do."

Lorraine chuckled. "You make it sound okay."

Nelson took the remote control from Lorraine. He pressed the power button. "You've given up a lot. But it can't be compared to what you've given to people. Not just the cases you hear but the people like Terry and myself you gave a second chance. I won't speak for anyone else but I know you're a good person. What they're accusing you of is ridiculous. I'll testify to that."

Lorraine looked into Nelson's eyes. She remembered the day she interviewed him for the position. Everything about him said don't hire me. His criminal record caused many people to run the other way, but Lorraine knew firsthand the loyalty people assigned individuals who gave them a second chance. Her smile put him at ease. "Thank you, Nelson. We may have to take you up on that."

"I'm ready when you are." Nelson smiled.

Chapter 8

....

WITNESS HUMILIATION

....

Eight Days Later; Courthouse

Prosecutor Scribner approached the witness stand with a smile. "The prosecution calls Terry Johnson to the stand."

Lorraine gasped.

Tristan looked at the paperwork and shook his head. "Terry Johnson is listed as a witness for the prosecution."

Lorraine shook her head.

Terry took slow steps to the witness stand.

Time stood still.

Lorraine cleared her throat.

Scribner turned and smirked at Lorraine.

Lorraine crossed her arms. "This is unreal."

"Keep calm the truth is on your side." Tristan whispered to Lorraine.

"Your honor, the state requests permission to treat the witness as hostile." Scribner approached Judge Light's bench.

"Be reminded this is an evidentiary hearing. Permission granted." Judge Light nodded.

"Please state your name." The Prosecutor blocked Terry's view of Lorraine.

"Terry Johnson." Terry's throat felt dry as the Sahara.

"What was your prison identification number?" Scribner smiled at Terry.

"I don't remember."

Scribner looked at the Judge. "You expect Judge Light and the rest of this court to believe you've forgotten a number used to identify you for the better part of the last ten years."

Terry shrugged.

"The witness is instructed to answer." Judge Light gave an empathetic look to Terry.

"658749715." Terry's arms crossed.

"Thank you." Scribner said.

"How long have you known Judge Allen?" Scribner switched to the opposite side of the witness stand, giving Terry the ability to see Lorraine.

"I've known her as long as I've been free." Terry said.

"Technically, you're not free. You were given a provisional early release. If it is shown you've engaged in any improper behavior you'll be sent back to the prison to finish your sentence." Scribner smiled.

"Ask a question or allow the defense to cross examine." Judge Light said.

"Yes, your honor." Scribner said. "How long since you were released?"

"Three years."

Scribner's retrieved a file folder from the table. A copy was passed to Judge Light, Terry and Tristan.

Lorraine leaned over and looked over Tristan's shoulder as he opened it and read through several pages. Certain sections were highlighted, marked and underlined.

"Please tell the court what you're holding." Scribner blocked Terry's view of Lorraine.

"They are copies of letters between Judge Allen and myself." Terry said.

"Please tell the court how many years it's been since the date of the first letter." Scribner said.

"Five years." Terry said just above a whisper.

"So you lied." Scribner turned around and pointed at Lorraine. "You've known Judge Allen for more than three years."

"No, I've only known her since I was released. Saying you know someone you write letters with as part of a program to satisfy a requirement to complete a rehabilitation program is like saying you're close personal friends with four thousand people on Facebook." Terry chuckled.

"Is this funny, to you, Terry?" Scribner approached the witness stand.

"The trial, no. That question, a little." Terry leaned forward. "Can I go back to my seat now?"

"Not yet. I've highlighted and pasted sections of the letters between you and Judge Allen that are not appropriate to be read aloud. Please confirm that you wrote and received these letters." Scribner clicked on the projector.

Every head in the courtroom turned. Quiet occupied the thick air. Several gasps added to the tension in the room.

"Yes. But..." Terry leaned forward.

Scribner raised her hand to cut Terry's words off. "No further question. I request that we recess until tomorrow to read the rest of the correspondence outlined and I continue questioning tomorrow morning."

Judge Light looked through the thick folder. "Agreed. Court will reconvene tomorrow afternoon at 1PM."

Scribner walked past the table and winked at Lorraine.

Tristan studied the papers in the file.

Lorraine frowned.

"We need to go over these letters, this doesn't look good, Lorraine."

"It's not what it looks like, Tristan, I swear." Lorraine shook her head.

"I hope not, because this looks bad."

***

Sunday: Terry Johnson's

Mrs. Johnson stormed through the front door. She stomped into the living room where Terry watched football with Terrance. They looked up from the game. Terry's head pointed toward the kitchen.

"I've never been so humiliated in all of my life. Have you any idea what they are saying about you all over the world?" Mrs. Johnson huffed.

Terry's eyebrows raised.

"Don't pretend you don't know what I'm talking about. I thought you were upfront and honest with me about the things you said happened with your boss before you were released. She used her influence to get you the provisional release with no parole payments. That should've tipped me off you were doing something perverted. You're just like your father." Mrs. Johnson swore.

Terry leaned forward. Hand swiped down over face in quick movements. "I'm tired of being compared to him every time I do something you don't approve. If our presence here is so cumbersome, I'll be glad to pack me, my boy and leave."

"No you won't remember, his custody reverted to me when you were taken into the state's custody and until you're really free he'll be mine." Mrs. Johnson sneered. "So you are free to leave but he stays, he is mine."

"No, I'm sure that some of the good stuff from his Daddy and some of the positive stuff from my Dad is what have kept him from following in my footsteps. I recall a colorful past you like to pretend never existed that assigned state ID to you long before I was a twinkle in my father's eye. He may have been married but no one forced you to sleep with him." Terry sneered.

"You've never let me forget my imperfections before I married your stepfather. One moment I attempted to be honest with you to try to get you off that path of degradation you refused to leave and now you throw it into my face." Mrs. Johnson swiped at her face.

"I never asked that creep for anything he gave me and newsflash mommy dearest, it wasn't my degradation that landed me with matching prison numbers to you. Your sonny boy is the one I covered for so he wouldn't lose his precious future. No one not you or Mr. Johnson ever thought to ask how we were both in the same place at the same time but I arrived home a full hour before him." Terry turned toward the wall. The promise to a dead sibling to carry the secret felt too heavy to bear with the other pressures mounting up in court.

"Stop that. Don't say that." Mrs. Johnson's head shook.

Terry looked into Mrs. Johnson's face. "You know already, don't you? Most criminals are pretty smart. The story never added up to anyone except that stupid cop. I never did what they accused me of, we just never had to put as much effort into making sure dumb Terry, the mistake from Mommy's past was given any more opportunity than a raggedy new last name from a deadbeat cretin."

"Don't disrespect my late husband. He left this house and what little savings I have is from him, when he passed." Mrs. Johnson sniffed.

Terry sat at the table. "Aren't you forgetting the money left over after you buried your golden boy, the promised child, the gifted one?"

Mrs. Johnson shook her head as tears streamed down her face. "Why are you doing this?"

"I'm tired of you pretending I'm the black omen hovering over this family. My biological father visited me in prison and told me about everything. He kept money on my books and he pulled the strings to help me get early release. All Lorraine did was help me find him. We wrote about it in my letters and that moronic prosecutor is twisting everything around." Terry trembled with anger. "I'm not sure what is going on but I'm going to get to the bottom of it, I'm tired of everyone using me as their patsy. My scapegoat days are done."

"First they harass me, whisper about me and treat me like a leper at church and then I come home to this, what a great way to spend the Lord's Day." Mrs. Johnson wept into her hands.

"You should be focused on God if it is the Lord's Day, not how those hypocrites in some old decrepit building treat you. People who care about you won't take the word of slick reporters, talking heads, and gossip blogs over you. Stop thinking about them and focus on your faith." Terry stood.

"Focus on my faith?" Mrs. Johnson wiped her face.

"Yes." Terry walked toward the living room and paused in the door. "If something this small compared to the big God you preached to me about in those letters is real, something as small as people's opinions shouldn't stop you from having faith in Him. Not if you were there every Sunday for Him, instead of those people or you."

***

Lorraine sipped the honey chamomile vanilla tea from her favorite mug. Newspaper headlines, blogpost titles and sound bites from the press about the latest development in the case tortured her. The solitude and loneliness that drove her to pursue membership in the circle and purchase the mountain cabin for entertaining her new cohorts, soothed her. All of the lies and frustrations of the case Scribner continued to mount caused Lorraine to question her decisions.

The doorbell rang. Lorraine checked her phone. Nelson left and planned to spend time with his children today, so she had no idea who it could be. She gasped when she saw the man standing on her porch. Her front door flew open before she could catch her breath.

He turned around with a smile. His calm youthful countenance grew into quiet confidence. She moved to the side so he could enter the home they once shared. "Good morning, Dyson."

"Good morning, Lorraine. I talked to Yvonne and she sends her regards." Dyson smiled. He took a seat on the couch.

"Tell her and your children, I said hello." Lorraine sat in the chair across from her ex-husband.

"Your trial is all over the news and I know this must be causing great anxiety for you. Your career means so much to you." Dyson relaxed against the couch.

Regret covered her. Questions about the decision to live her life to leave a legacy instead of giving her love to the best man she met her entire life. Things she felt were best for her six months ago, appeared to be the worst things for her.

"Lorraine, did you hear me?" Dyson said.

"It did. It does. Nothing I held in high esteem is as important as I believed. There are so many things I've lost and am sure I'll never have again. Once this trial is over, I'm sure that I'll get back to what I do best, which is helping people using the law." Lorraine sipped from her mug and placed it on the table in front of her.

"You want me to believe that you, Lorraine 'Always Wanted to Be a Judge' Allen is questioning if you should have dedicated your life to more than law. There is a God..." Dyson chuckled.

Lorraine gave him a half smile.

"You're serious." Dyson's face dropped. "Whoa."

"No one is more surprised by how much I've been questioning my decisions over the weekend than I am. Giving up the love of my life, chance at motherhood and family time has proven to be one of the most confusing decisions I've ever made." Lorraine sighed. "Maybe it's the tea talking."

"Greatness of any kind comes at a cost. No one whose impacted the lives of others has done so without paying a hefty price. Been that way since Moses." Dyson leaned forward. "You're being too hard on yourself. It's not too late to change the direction your life is going."

"Moses Stewart, from our graduating high school class? What does he have to do with anything?" Lorraine looked perplexed.

Dyson laughed again. "Lorraine, you're priceless. I love my wife and she is an amazing woman but I'm glad for the time we had together too. You showed me how to lay it all on the line for what you want. When our marriage dissolved, I was devastated. It took years, prayers, and tears but I realized things about myself in the face of our failed relationship I may have never learned if we'd have stayed together."

"I'm afraid I don't follow you."

"You gave up everything for your career. I don't believe the allegations, I know your tastes. What they're saying," Dyson shook his head, "Terry isn't your cup of tea. Don't believe for one minute that you've been as perfect as the society columns suggest but I know who you are at the core of your being well enough to know you wouldn't jeopardize everything you worked for in order to explore something you know you wouldn't like. I believe in you, maybe God is using this as a wake up call. He wants to make you aware that there is more to life."

"Our marriage failing, did that for you? It made you a better person. How?" Lorraine shook her head.

"Because it forced me to face my worst fear, the dream I'd concocted in my mind was destroyed. No two point five children. No white picket fence. No dog. There was no one but me to look back at myself and who I really was instead of who I believed myself to be. It forced me to grow up and take responsibility for the man I was so I could become the man, I am. Failure was the catalyst for my success, not as a professor but as a person." Dyson smiled.

Lorraine nodded. "You think all of this happening could be for a reason and make me a better person. Not a better judge, but a better woman?"

Dyson nodded.

"Interesting. I don't know if I agree but it is a better thing to consider than the alternative."

"Which would be?"

"That I gave up everything and everyone precious to me, to pursue something worthless." Lorraine fought back tears. She blinked. "I can't bear thinking my life may have had more meaning by doing less than climbing the ladder of success."

"Well, I'll tell Yvonne you said, hi." Dyson stood. "She's been praying for you, everyone really in the trial."

Lorraine nodded. "Thanks. I think Terry needs it more than I do. My name isn't the only one being dragged through the mud. First a false conviction, dead brother and now the possibility of losing it all, again. I'd be a basket case already."

"Sounds like Terry had intercessors, before all this began. I'll be sure we add Terry's name to the list. Call me if you need anything." Dyson motioned for Lorraine to walk him to the door.

Lorraine followed him with a sigh. "Thank you, words can't explain how much I needed this visit. Just didn't know I did."

"That is what family is for." Dyson hugged Lorraine and walked out of the door.

Chapter 9

THE BRIEFCASE

Trial Resumes; Courthouse

"Defense, your case." Judge Light said. He nodded toward Tristan.

"I'd like to invoke my option to recall Sidney Smead to the stand." Tristan leaned on his table.

Sidney Smead's eyes squinted until they disappeared.

Tristan smiled. "Please state your name again."

"Sidney Smead and your brother is Anthony Smead?" Tristan nodded to someone and the courts doors opened.

A tall man with broad shoulders, dark hair and piercing green eyes entered the court.

Lorraine sighed.

Tristan winked at her.

Sidney's face changed colors three times.

Scribner turned around with a huff.

"So you testified that you worked for Judge Allen during the summer after your probation. Is that correct?" Tristan opened a file on the table next to Lorraine.

Sidney's fingers strummed a rhythm on the side arm of the chair. "If that's what I said."

"So it would be safe to assume you never worked for Judge Allen?" Tristan pulled two pieces of paper.

"Maybe you need to get your ears checked." Sidney laughed.

"No, my hearing is fine as well as my investigative skills." Silence filled the room as Tristan handed a piece of paper to Scribner and Judge Light. "Those investigative skills helped me secure your arrest record... Your blank arrest record. I've never seen anyone with such a squeaky clean record. Not so much as a parking ticket since you graduated from junior college. Tell me how it is you came to work for Judge Allen after you were paroled from--the pretend penitentiary?"

Scribner turned red.

Lorraine smiled.

Anthony stood. "Sidney!"

Sidney looked down at the floor in front of the witness stand.

"Do you have a response?" Judge Light looked at Scribner and Tristan.

Sidney tried to make eye contact with Scribner.

"Please answer Mr. Reeves." Judge Light looked at Sidney.

"I'll repeat the question. You testified that you worked for Judge Allen. Please tell the court what really happened the summer you claimed to work for Judge Allen." Tristan stood in front of the witness.

Sidney sighed. "Nothing happened. Lorraine was involved with Anthony for the first half of the year into the summer. He wanted to pursue a relationship. She turned him down because she was too focused on her career. She ran him out of town."

Tristan nodded. "No further questions."

"This is not an official trial but lying during this investigation is going to ruin that perfect record of yours." Judge Light said. "See the bailiff after you exit the witness stand."

"I can explain." Sidney looked at Judge Light.

Scribner stood. "I object. The defense has released the witness. We need time to go over the papers presented as evidence."

"Please step down." Judge Light said.

Sidney stepped down.

"Prosecution requests a recess until tomorrow." Scribner's face turned red.

Judge Light looked at Tristan. "Defense has no objection."

Lorraine touched Tristan's elbow.

"I'm calling Terry tomorrow. We need more time to prepare." Tristan whispered.

"Fine. We recess until first thing tomorrow morning." Judge Light slammed his gavel.

***

Lorraine sat in the booth across from Tristan. "Please tell me what happened. You could have nailed Scribner to the wall with those signed affidavits from two of her witnesses they paid to lie about their accusations against me."

"Lorraine, I have to ask you a question. Do you know anything about all of this circle stuff they've been talking about on the news?"

Color drained from Lorraine's cheeks.

Tristan swallowed. "The answer isn't as important as your answer to this question. Do you know why God has allowed any of this to happen? When Scribner requested the recess, I knew I should allow them time to look over the papers because that is the right thing to do. We have Anthony Smead here to counter if Sidney would have continued to lie but his testimony wasn't necessary."

Lorraine nodded.

"Don't answer me now. Go home and think about everything this trial can cost you and ask yourself if what you've given up for your career is worth it. I don't know all the details but I know there is something you haven't been telling me during this trial. When I pray for you--"

Lorraine's eye bucked. "You pray for me?"

"I pray for all of my clients, Lorraine. You're no exception to them in that regard. They may all have other things they've been accused of, most of them are even guilty, but that doesn't mean they don't deserve a second chance." Tristan sipped water from a water bottle. "Is there any reason to believe Terry is going to get on the stand and lie for them tomorrow?"

Lorraine shook her head. "Of course not. Terry is the most honest person I know."

"I wonder how many people would have said the same thing about Sidney Smead?" Tristan sighed.

***

Eternity; Throne of Grace

"She is a hopeless case. Why waste anymore time on her? You sent Dyson, his wife is praying for her and she still refuses to acknowledge You. Let it go. She doesn't want to and never will know You. Give me what is mine, I want her soul." Satan paced back and forth before the Father.

"Silence." The Father said just above a whisper. "You're a liar, and birthing every lie that is being used to attempt to crush her and Terry. You've been given all the access to her you'll have unless you have something new to ask leave my presence."

Satan paused. He looked at the Father then the Son and smirked. "Yes, Master, I'll go finish my job and next time we talk about Lorraine Allen it'll be when You banish her to hell with me for eternity."

"Go." The Son said.

Satan disappeared.

"Father, he's right, she still hasn't accepted Our love, please help Me help those fighting for her in the heavenly realm. The angels reported that the enemy has doubled his efforts and she is under constant torment. Disgusting dreams, lusting in her flesh, nightmares and her mind. He is using her gifts, the gift of her intelligence and creativity You gave her against her. Let Me release the special legion of angels assigned to fight these kinds of battles on her behalf. Yvonne has requested special angelic hosts to be released and her heart is open and pure toward Us. Please, Father, they need help."

"Only for Lorraine?" The Father looked in the Son's eyes.

"No, We need special warriors for all of them, especially Terry. The attack the enemy has planned to compromise all the prayers and work to show Our love in this situation has taken its toll and

Terry needs to be protected like never before. May I give the order to release the tactical warriors? There is not much time before the enemy delivers his greatest blow. If We don't have them in position the Intercessors and Evangelists may not be able to reach Lorraine and Terry at the exact moments We need them to, please, Father."

The Father motioned toward an angel that appeared to blend into the background. "All you've heard Him say, make it happen for them. Go now, pierce the fabric of time and do whatever you have to do to make sure everyone is in their right place to cover them, especially Lorraine and Terry."

"Yes, Master." The angel said. He turned and soared toward the spiritual realm entrance the messenger angels used when they asked for help from the Lord.

***

The case of beer felt like lead in Terry's hand. Distance from the driveway to the front door felt like five hundred miles instead of fifty feet. Judge Allen's case appeared almost over, but her lawyer looked primed and ready for the kill. Terry knew all too well how much lawyer's wanted to win. No matter who or what it cost. Each year in jail ingrained how much lawyers wanted to win for their client into Terry's mind.

Footsteps behind Terry halted progress to the front door. Terry turned around. The sound stopped. "I know you're back there. Unless you want some serious damage done to you I suggest you come out."

Silence replied to Terry. Energy from somewhere propelled Terry to the door. Keys turned the lock. The beer found its way into the refrigerator.

"Some weird people been fiddling around here. They trying to look like they belong. You know how the neighborhood is, they stick out like cowlicks." Mrs. Johnson sat across from Terry. "I'm tired, Terry. You caught a bad rap. Looking back over things these past few weeks since the people at the church stopped talking to me, I see the error in how I treated you. Not sure what I could ever do to make it up to you, but for what it's worth, I'm"

Someone pounded on the door.

"Terrance, go upstairs to your room." Terry moved as if the stress of the day didn't weigh a ton in the driveway.

Mrs. Johnson stepped into the foyer with the .38 pistol. She nodded.

"Who is it?" Terry pushed the window back.

A tall woman holding a briefcase accompanied the giant that visited them from Scribner's camp.

Terry inched the door open. "What do you want?"

"Can you let us in please?" The woman wore her nervousness like makeup.

With a shrug, Terry stepped back to allow them into the foyer.

Mrs. Johnson nodded. She made no attempt to hide her gun.

The giant nodded at Terry and Mrs. Johnson. "Evening ma'am."

"What can I do for you?" Terry sighed.

The woman took tentative steps toward Mrs. Johnson. "Excuse me, ma'am."

Mrs. Johnson took a few steps toward Terry.

Something shiny glistened under the giants suit jacket.

Terry and Mrs. Johnson exchanged a glance.

"I told you everything you needed to know last time and nothing has changed. You're lying about me and Judge Allen. Simple." Terry shrugged. "Now have a good evening."

"Even if this is settled and Judge Allen isn't removed from the bench. She won't be reappointed. How are you going to make a living? No one else will hire you because of your record. Your son and mother are glad to have you home. Our circle of friends have the same if not more connections than Judge Allen. Cooperate with us and we'll have your parole made permanent and compensate you for your trouble." The woman placed the suitcase on the table in the foyer. She opened it and revealed stacks of money.

"Whoa." Terrance said from the stairs.

"Go back upstairs." Terry didn't turn to look at him.

"We're taking the money, right?" Terrance didn't move.

Terry turned around. "GO BACK UPSTAIRS!"

Mrs. Johnson inched toward the suitcase. She fingered the stacks and looked at Terry. "Saints alive. I don't think I ever believed that much money really existed."

Terry turned to the woman. "I'm not for sale."

"The first million is for your trouble, Terry. The rest is considered a relocation fee. We don't want to buy you. Just testify that what we said happened is true. You and Judge Allen were lovers, you and Judge Allen didn't go to the cabin to work on cases, it was your love chateau. You're worth more than a few dollars. We're simply paying to alter your memory." The woman nodded at the giant.

The giant closed the suitcase and stood it next to the small table.

Terry stared at the suitcase without blinking.

"What are you going to do?" Terrance said, from the staircase.

"Get out of my house…" Terry said. "…Before I change my mind. Leave."

The woman nodded at the man. "Have a good evening."

Mrs. Johnson closed the door as the man and woman left. "Terry, what are you going to do with all of that money?"

Terry looked at her. "What do you think I'm going to do? Did you hear what they said? Even if Judge Allen beats this, if I don't testify against her, when I lose my job I go back to jail."

"They don't know that, they just want to win." Mrs. Johnson paced back and forth. "You saw what happened to the others who lied on her. This is serious."

"I think you should do it. We can all relocate somewhere they can never find us with one million dollars. She said it was more than one million. " Terrance came down the stairs.

Terry turned to face Terrance. Whatever happened to his entire moral code, future decisions and mindset rested on the decision to lie or not lie on the stand in less than twenty four hours.

Mrs. Johnson looked at Terry.

Terry picked up the suitcase. "I have to make a run. You guys stay here and don't answer the door for anyone."

"Not even, Jesus." Terrance laughed.

"He is known for making ways into houses with no open doors." Terry smiled at Mrs. Johnson.

"What?" Terrance looked puzzled.

"Ask your grandmother." Terry kissed Mrs. Johnson on the cheek. "I'll be back."

Mrs. Johnson wiped tears from her eyes with a nod.

***

Twenty Four Hours Later

Lorraine pulled on her suit jacket. The trial day didn't start for four hours but her eyes popped open at five in the morning and refused to close. Thoughts of her early days practicing law filled her mind. Happy moments with Dyson. Stressful moments with Dyson. Final moments with Dyson. She sacrificed everything for her career, turned her back on everything and everyone who couldn't serve her ambitions.

Her kitchen sparkled like new. Time at home allowed her to rearrange it the way she promised to herself the second year after Dyson moved out. All the things she promised to do later, she'd done while she waited to find out if she would be able to continue to build her legacy. A legacy now marred with the scandal of wrong choices and bad company. She traded the truth of love, family and patience for the lie of instant gratification. The rumors about the circle didn't entice her but the acceleration to her career plans made her inquire about the married side of it.

Dyson looked at her as if her skin peeled back from her face when she tried to test his interest in walking on the wild side in their bedroom, with other couples. After losing her third case to a litigator she knew participated in the sex parties the circle held, she started formulating an exit plan from her marriage. Love for Dyson was dwarfed by her thirst for power, influence and success.

The timer on the coffee maker alerted her to the full cup waiting for her consumption. Her thoughts led her toward a place in her heart she dared not enter often. She flipped on the television. Regret filled her as her most recent headshot sat behind Scott Lovitt's well manicured profile.

"Good Morning. Scott Lovitt, with a breaking insider video showing what is alleged to be Judge Lorraine Allen hosting a party for her secret sex society. She has been rumored to be the regional leader of the society responsible for her being appointed to her seat on the bench. Here is a snippet. We'll play the entire video later today after our full in five." Scott Lovitt nodded.

The first five seconds of the video played in court occupied her television screen. Before rage was able to fill Lorraine, she noticed something in the frame she missed when it was played in the courtroom. Unable to contain her excitement she squealed as her feet carried her full speed into her library. A conversation with Terry about being too organized caused her to laugh out loud. There nestled between two other media cards full of recordings of company holiday parties sat the video that would blow the entire case against her and Terry out of the water.

Lorraine tucked it into her suit jacket. A smile filled her face as she pulled her smart phone from her pocket. Tristan's number sat on top of her recent call list. She pressed the call button.

"Hello." A groggy filled voice said.

"Um..I'm sorry. I didn't realize it was so early. Tristan?" Lorraine made her way back to her kitchen.

"Good morning, Judge Allen." Tristan sighed. "Is everything okay?"

"It is. Better than okay. Scott Lovitt aired the video from the trial today and I noticed something that I have in my own videos from my cabin that can prove that the party they showed wasn't at my cabin."

The sounds of someone moving around eked through the speaker of the phone. Tristan cleared his throat. "Really?"

"I can show it to you. We could meet at the coffeehouse near the court." Lorraine said.

"We don't have time for that. I believe you, get a copy to my house as soon as you can and I'll meet you in court. I'm texting the address to you right now." Tristan laughed. "God works in mysterious ways."

"If you say so. I'll believe it when He works all of this out and I don't lose everything I've worked for otherwise I'll stick to my current views on God." Lorraine chuckled.

"What are those? I didn't know you had any view." Tristan said.

"I don't." Silence filled the space between them. "I'll have the simm card to you in fifteen minutes no more than half an hour."

"This conversation isn't over, Judge Allen." Tristan said.

"I'm open to finishing it as long as that is what people continue to call me." Lorraine pressed end.

Chapter 10

....

MONEY, POWER, RESPECT

....

Scribner stood as the office door opened and closed. A woman walked in smiling. "So?"

The woman nodded. "Everything is done."

"Good." Scribner smiled. "This is going to be so fun to watch. If I weren't me, I'd want to be me so I could watch her face fall when her little protégé drops the bomb."

The woman gave Scribner a weird look.

"We're done. I have to prepare for court." Scribner reached for the phone and waved the woman away. "Was there something else, you needed?"

"My payment wasn't in the envelope." She crossed her arms with hand extended palm up.

"That S.O.B. who I assigned to protect you and the money was supposed to ...Never mind." Scribner opened a drawer. Three stacks of banded twenty dollar bills landed on the desk in front of the woman.

She picked it up. Her eyebrow raised. "We agreed on four,"

"Bonus, for a job well done." Scribner winked at her.

She winked back. "You let me know if there is anything else I can do for you."

The phone found its way back into the cradle. "Now that you mention it, there is one other thing I need help with."

The woman smiled. "Yes."

"Meet me back here after the trial this evening to discuss it further." Scribner smacked the woman on the backside as she walked out of the room. The sound of ringing on the phone stopped.

"Hello." A woman said.

"Terry is playing for our side now." Scribner laughed. "We should be swearing you into her bench and the circle should be in full swing again this time next week."

A throaty laugh came through the phone. "I'm so excited, we should ditch the circle. Together we'd be unstoppable. Heat from the press is too much for it to be safe, for now."

Scribner laughed. "That makes it even better, doll. We'll be fine. You just meet me at my office tonight ready to celebrate. I'll have a surprise waiting for you."

"You do know how to keep a girl happy. I love surprises. See you then." The line clicked.

"Too bad, Lorraine never found out. But she will show everyone else, it's just better to give me what I want." Scribner turned the lights off and exited the room.

***

Tristan turned to the Judge then the court for dramatic effect.

Lorraine sat up so straight she looked two inches taller.

"Your honor," Tristan turned to face Judge Light. "With your permission I'd like to show the footage introduced into the evidence by Special Prosecutor Scribner."

Judge Light nodded. "Proceed."

Tristan turned to the court's a/v technician. The sounds for the party roared through the speakers as the scenes of a wild party played out on the wall. "Please pause the video at the frame I instructed."

The a/v technician nodded. A shot of the windowsill and fireplace mantle froze on the screen.

Lorraine looked over at Scribner with a smile.

Scribner fidgeted with papers on the table. Every eye in the court room focused on the stand alone projector.

"Thank you, please play the second video. Please stop in the places I showed you." Tristan said.

The film rolled and an almost identical room showed on the screen. The date in the corner of the video was the same day as the other video. Pictures on the wall were different and the design of the room showed that they were not the same location. A picture of Judge Allen sat where an art deco print sat over the fireplace in the first video.

Position of the window in contrast to the fireplace also showed that they were not facing the sun in the same way. Sunlight streamed into the room from the opposite direction of the original video. Tristan nodded. The a/v technician paused the video in a shot similar to the one on the original video.

"There is nothing illegal happening in either of these frames. Judge Light has been informed of the believed owner of the initial cabin by Judge Allen but the footage shows that these cabins are not the same. We have signed affidavits from employees, friends and the maintenance crew that the decor in Judge Allen's cabin has been unchanged since she purchased it months before this video was created." Tristan smiled at Lorraine.

Lorraine nodded.

"Please turn the screens off." Tristan turned to face Judge Light. "We'd like to call our next witness. Former Commissioner of County Waste, Alvin Dunn."

Alvin Dunn took nervous steps toward the witness stand. A bailiff spoke with Mr. Dunn and he took his seat.

"Mr. Dunn, you resigned from your elected position of Commissioner of County Waste several months ago citing personal reasons. Is that correct?"

Mr. Dunn wiped sweat from his brow. He leaned forward. "Yes."

"Is there any particular reason you stepped down from the position?" Tristan stood in front of Mr. Dunn so he could not see the prosecution.

"To save my marriage." Mr. Dunn wiped his brow again.

"Most wives are happy, proud of their husbands when they're elected as civil servants. Your wife wanted you to quit your position. Why?" Tristan said.

"She found out I was a member of 'The Circle' and told me she wanted me to leave it and everything associated with it or she was leaving me and taking our kids back to live with her parents." Mr. Dunn stared at the ground.

Murmurs filled the courtroom.

Judge Light banged his gavel. "Order."

"Mr. Dunn, were you one of the masked men in that footage?" Tristan indicated the first video.

Mr. Dunn nodded.

"For the records please answer verbally," Tristan said.

"Yes, " Mr. Dunn cleared his throat. "I was the masked marauder. There were many of us there, because we wanted to be there, and Lorraine. Excuse me, Judge Allen was not one of us."

"You're saying you didn't see Judge Allen at this party?" Tristan said.

"I never encountered Judge Allen at all during my time in 'The Circle." Mr. Dunn said.

"Thank you." Tristan turned to Scribner. "No further questions."

Prosecutor Scribner took several long moments to approach the witness stand.

"Mr. Dunn, you were a voluntary member of this group. Did you know all of the members?" Scribner looked down at the man as sweat poured down his face.

"No." Mr. Dunn croaked. His voice cracked. "Excuse me. No, you moved up and around in it as your career advanced."

"So it is possible, you and Lorraine weren't in the same parties because you weren't on her level? Is that what you're saying, sir?" Prosecutor Scribner spat the last word out as if it was a swallowed bug.

Mr. Dunn looked down at the floor. "Yes."

"No further questions for this," Scribner's voice dropped, "witness."

Tristan stood. "I'd like to recall Terry Johnson to the stand."

***

Terry walked to the stand in record speed.

"You're still under oath from before." Judge Light said.

"Yes sir." Terry relaxed against the back of the chair.

"Please state your full name for the court." Tristan said.

"Terry Johnson."

"How long have you been working for Judge Allen?" Tristan looked at Lorraine.

"A little over three years." Terry looked at the prosecutors table.

"How did you come to know, Judge Allen?" Tristan turned around and faced the witness stand.

"She spoke at my college graduation ceremony and invited us to write to her. I did. We became pen pals." Terry said.

"The letters that Prosecutor Scribner referenced earlier. Would you like to elaborate on the sections she had you read from?"

"Yes. Those letters were about a novel series we were reading together. One of the things Judge Allen recommended I do. She said she needed to read more for recreation too. So, we started reading the New York Times best seller lists together. The sections highlighted were direct quotes from the book that we pulled as references to talk about certain things in the series. It was a trilogy about this married couple and their affairs." Terry took a deep breath.

Tristan walked back to the table. A uniformed police officer entered the courtroom. He motioned for Tristan to meet him at his table. "Your Honor, may I have a moment."

"Very brief, Mr. Reeves."

The officer huddled with Tristan at the table next to Lorraine. Tristan nodded quickly several times. "Your Honor, we have new evidence that needs to be introduced pertaining to this witness. I ask your permission for the officer to approach the bench."

"Proceed." Judge Light leaned forward.

The officer carried the briefcase, handcuffed to his wrist, to the bench. He placed it in front of the judge and handed a slip of paper to Tristan. Tristan read the paper. "Defense presents this affidavit from the city that the contents of this briefcase is 1.5 million dollars in unmarked bills."

"Terry, can you tell us the contents of this briefcase?" Tristan said.

"It's a bribe to testify that Judge Allen and I are lovers instead of coworkers." Terry looked at Lorraine. "Which is not true. Judge Allen is my boss and a friend. That is all. I didn't even count it. Didn't want to be tempted. After they left I took it to the police."

All color drained from Prosecutor Scribner's face.

A gasp went up in the courtroom.

Judge Light banged his gavel. "Order!, Until further notice, this case is suspended again until we get to the bottom of this."

Tristan returned to the table. He sat next to Lorraine.

Scribner and the entire prosecution section scurried like rats from the courtroom.

Everyone except for Lorraine and Tristan exited the courtroom.

Lorraine looked at Tristan with tears running down her face. "I didn't know. How did you know? What just happened?"

"God just moved in a mysterious way. Judge Allen now the ball is in your court, no pun intended." Tristan stood. "Let's go get a bite to eat. Watching God work gives me quite the appetite."

Lorraine looked at him and shook her head. "The trial isn't over yet. What if they can't find the person who bribed Terry? These people are not normal. I used to be one of them. Trust me, the lengths they'll go to get what they want are immeasurable."

"That may be so. But that doesn't change the truth."

"What truth is that?" Lorraine stood.

"God's reach will always be farther than they're capable of going. When He is for you, nothing and no one can stand against you." Tristan smiled. "Now let's go eat."

Chapter 11

FIX IT

Senator Blythe, Alderman Holt, Judge Carver, Dr. Shields and Prosecutor Scribner crammed into the small office where Scribner planned to celebrate victory with two luscious women. The men all looked at each other then across the desk at Scribner. Scribner returned their stare with a false bravado practiced since law school. "Gentleman, this is a slight setback. Nothing major. We can handle this."

"Are you nuts? The jig is up. First the 'Circle' is busted up and now half a million dollars is missing and you want us to believe you have everything under control. We should have never let you talk us into this." Senator Blythe laughed. "You're nuts!"

"I hope you get some help with your emotional issues while you're locked up. If you cooperate I'm sure they'll send you to a minimum security facility, something with a golf course." Dr. Shields smiled.

"Don't start with me, Shields. We'll get this taken care of. As soon as I hunt that trumpet who told me everything was solid down, I'll handle it. She was supposed to meet me here that evening. Of course, she didn't show up. This was all over the news. We should have kept someone on Terry to make sure this wouldn't happen. An honest criminal. How was I supposed to plan for that?" Scribner's head shook. "I can't believe this."

"What about the money? How do you explain that there is a half a million dollars missing?" Alderman Holt said.

"Terry testified that the money went straight to the police after our people left. Terry was too afraid to count it and stay honest. Coward. What is wrong with this country when you can't bribe someone with two million, even one and a half million dollars?" Scribner scowled.

"Are you serious? This is bigger than just some money. If they find them before we do. We could all be facing time. Scribner you started this, now you fix it." Senator Blythe said. He grabbed Scribner's face and pulled it within inches of his own. "Use all of those looks and charms to get this taken care of or the job being filled will be yours. They'll have a field day with that pretty face of yours in prison."

Scribner smacked Blythe's hand away. "Back up. I've got this under control. Don't worry."

Judge Carver's phone beeped. He pulled it from its holster on his waist. "You've got to be kidding me. Turn on the television."

Scribner found the remote and powered up a twenty-inch flat screen television on the wall.

The woman who delivered the money to Terry was being handcuffed at the bus station. A police officer shoved her head into the back of a squad car. Scott Lovitt's face appeared from the side of the screen. "Breaking news in what now appears to be the staged scandal of the honorable Lorraine Allen. Sketch artist put together a composite from the Johnson family and a bus driver alerted authorities to her presence on his bus this afternoon headed to California. We'll keep you informed with any new developments. Authorities are hoping to get the source of the bribe and other details from the suspect to bring the case against Judge Allen to a close or proceed."

Scribner blinked. "Judge Carver, I know you're enjoying this since Lorraine was one of your favorite playmates, but do you think you could arrange to get a message to the prisoner? If not we'll all be sharing a table in court."

Judge Carver gulped. "This is the last favor, Scribner."

"Thank you, Your Honor." Scribner smiled.

Dr. Shields and Senator Blythe exchanged a look.

"I'll be sure to keep that in mind once the Judge calls us back to court. Your confidence is overwhelming." Scribner said.

"We'll be keeping our distance from you as well. Between you and the media if we cough someone is gonna get a cheap thrill. I've never enjoyed that feeling, you remember that feeling, Scribner isn't that how you paid your way through law school?" Senator Blythe said.

"Of course, I remember, Walter. I also still have a record of all my best clients." Scribner looked around the room. "Now if you gentleman will excuse me, I have a mess to clean up."

Dr. Shields stood and leaned forward on the desk. "Make sure you clean it up well, this time, prosecutor. You cost all of us more than we bargained for when you went after Lorraine and if anything else goes wrong, there will be hell to pay."

"Don't threaten me, old man." Scribner laughed. "We know you miss playing with your buddy. Get over it. Maybe now you can make an honest woman out of her, the 'Circle' has been broken. Remember?"

"We're all aware of what you've done, Scribner. And two things you should know about this old man. I've got a long memory and I don't make threats. I deliver on promises." Dr. Shields stood. "Gentleman, let's leave, make good on our promise and put some distance between us and this sordid ordeal."

*****

Twelve Days Later
Lorraine's phone rang. "Hello."

"We'll be back in court tomorrow. They found the man the woman says gave her the money to bribe Terry face down in the landfill a few days ago, with two bullets to the temple from his own gun." Tristan said.

"Scribner is good. I know, someone got to that girl in county jail." Lorraine closed her eyes. "You have no idea how far the circle reached."

"We still have to talk." Tristan cleared his throat.

"The trial isn't over yet, Mr. Reeves." Lorraine said.

***

"Terry, did you take the briefcase to police headquarters that night?" Tristan said.

"It was a suitcase, but yes, I took the money to the cops." Terry nodded. "A woman and man came to my mother's home. They said they had at least one million reasons for me to say the allegations made against Judge Allen were true. This was after they attempted to scare me into testifying that what they said was true several days after the trial began."

"Why didn't you tell anyone about the intimidation attempts?" Tristan said.

"They said it would be the word of a convicted felon against a group of people with connections in Congress and I'd be smart to keep my mouth shut. I had no physical proof. So I did." Terry sighed. "Being in prison taught me when to know who to listen to, when they say shut up."

"Uh huh. Did the woman or man tell you the specific name of the person who sent them?" Tristan looked at Prosecutor Scribner's table.

"No. They didn't and I didn't ask. The heat he packed didn't give me the impression they were open to questions. I listened. Took the money and decided to turn it over because my son was studying me. He knows I was sent to prison under shaky circumstances and I didn't want him to think being crooked paid off in life. He has been through a lot since all of this has stayed in the news."

"So they didn't make any references to any one person or organization?" Tristan inched closer to the witness stand.

"They said, the circle they ran with had connections to make my parole permanent so I could leave town with the money. Higher than

Judge Allen." Terry leaned forward. "But Judge Allen didn't pull any strings for me. The warden selected me for the early release program because of my exemplary behavior while serving time."

Lorraine cleared her throat.

"And you stick to your previous testimony that you and Judge Lorraine Allen are nothing more than coworkers." Tristan said.

"No. I mean, yes." Terry sighed. "I'd like to believe we'd grown to be friends. At least while we were at work. She asked about my son, seemed genuine in her concern for my family. No one ever cared about me, the way she did."

Scribner's eyes reduced to slits and neck turned beet red.

"Defense rests, your honor." Tristan returned to the table and sat next to Lorraine.

"Redirect?" Judge Light looked at Scribner.

Through clenched teeth Scribner said, "No. Thank. You. Your. Honor."

"We'll take a brief recess for lunch and then I'll hear closing arguments." Judge Light tapped his gavel.

***

Scribner stood before the court with a tight smile. "We've come here to show that there is evidence of abuse of power, breach of contract and inappropriate conduct by a civil servant. Judge Lorraine Allen has been seen in many lights. No one has said she isn't a good community service volunteer or pen pal. The state has investigated and found proof that there have been all of the above mentioned actions by Judge Allen."

Scribner walked across the room and paused in front of Anthony Smead sitting two rows behind Vincent White. "While she has been in consenting May December romances and left the inexperienced men mesmerized with her antics and habits the court is not blind to her amoral ways. There is cause to utilize more taxpayer's funds to prosecute her to the fullest extent of the law. We'll prove she was a member and used her membership in the secret sex society to further her career aspirations including being appointed for her current position."

Tristan stood. He tugged on the bottom of his blazer. "I'm not saying that Judge Lorraine Allen is perfect. I'm not going to say that she hasn't been in what some consider to be less than upstanding personal arrangements. I am saying that the specific allegation she's been investigated regarding having a forced sexual relationship with her employee Terry Johnson is not true. It was so false, people who've yet to be identified paid over a million dollars to buy her guilt and because of her outstanding ability as a person, supervisor and friend Terry turned those funds over to the proper authorities. I ask that the evidence in this case be dismissed for what it is, nothing, and Judge Allen be allowed to return to the bench to serve her community."

"This case seemed open and shut day one. Nothing was further from the truth then and nothing is further from the truth today. I'll be looking over the case and rendering my decision first thing Monday. Court is recessed." Judge Light banged his gavel.

***

Exhaustion hit Terry hard as steel as the car rolled into the driveway. The desire to lay the driver seat back and nap in the car was stopped by the detective waiting on the porch. Detective Elliot from the night of the bribe.

Slow as molasses, Terry climbed out of the driver seat and approached the officer. "Good afternoon, Detective. How can I help you?"

Detective Elliot nodded. "Just needed to drop something off to you, if you have a moment. It would be safer if we talked inside."

Terry nodded and unlocked the front door.

"Are we alone?" Detective Elliot cocked his ear to the side.

"My mother and son are at her new church. I took him out of school after kids started to harass him about the trial." Terry shrugged. "So what do you need, Detective, I told you and the lawyers everything I know."

Detective pulled an envelope from his inside pocket. "This is a reward for coming forward to report the bribery attempt. Most people don't do the right thing anymore."

Terry thought about the look on the prosecutor's face when the amount was announced in court by Mr. Reeves. "How much was in the suitcase?"

Detective Reeves smiled. "I'm not at liberty to say. The accountant for the police station admitted 1.5 million into evidence."

Terry nodded.

"Well, that was all I needed." Detective Reeves took a step toward Terry. "May not seem like it was the right thing to do to some, but I couldn't shake the feeling that I needed to do this, you've been through a lot. I remember the case against you and what you did for your brother. He and I attended school together. Couldn't see you doing what they say you did."

Terry fought back tears. "That is because I didn't."

"I knew it." Detective Elliot smiled. "Well, maybe after all of this dies down, I'll see you around. Maybe we could go grab a drink."

Terry smiled. "Sounds good."

Chapter 12

THE VERDICT

Lorraine smoothed over the skirt, her favorite skirt. Her legs swung out of the driver's door. She wore this skirt the day they gave her the key to the city. Today it would become the skirt she wore the day she got her life back. Nothing went wrong when she wore this skirt.

Scribner slid into the passenger side door of Lorraine's car.

"Are you crazy? We're due in court in less than thirty minutes." Lorraine snatched the driver's side door shut.

"Let's do it. Right here. Right now. All I wanted was a chance to be with you. Everyone talked about you so much. I wanted to be a part of that." Scribner reached for Lorraine's hand near the armrest between them.

"You're certifiable. I'm not saying that as a joke. I believe you are in need of help from a psychiatric team." Lorraine snatched her hand back.

"You are the crazy one, who in their right mind doesn't want to get with all of this." Scribner said. "C'mon, Lorraine. You can be back on the bench this time tomorrow and we can reconstruct the 'Circle' more exclusive, powerful and steamy as ever. We could run it together."

"I don't want to be with you. I'm not into you or your type. You're taking this personal. Ask around, it's not my style. Paying my clerk one and a half million to lie about it should have tipped you off." Lorraine clicked the unlock button on the door.

"If you wanted to be attracted to me, you could. You never even tried." Scribner caressed Lorraine's knee. "I saw you and Terry together. Your legs wrapped around Terry's neck and the way you responded. Oh, you could be attracted to me if you wanted to be, Lorraine. I'd make you scream longer and harder than you did that weekend in the cabin and you'd love every minute of it."

"Okay, that is gross. I like what I like and you're not it. You lost, Scribner, go in this courtroom and take your beating like a man." Lorraine said.

"That's what I've been trying to do with you, but you won't let me." Scribner said. "We'll see if you're singing this same tune, when you lose."

Lorraine shook her head. "We should have been allies, instead you worked against me and exposed my dirt because you were in the same places doing dirt right along with me. You only broke the code because I played with someone better than I played with you. Every bone a dog buries is dug up at some point. I used to want to be there the day they unearthed yours, now I just feel sorry for you. Get out of my car and get some help."

***

Eternity; Throne of Grace

"The battle has heightened. The enemy has thrown everything he has into keeping her from confessing she accepts Our love." The Son stood.

"It will happen when it is time. We should rejoice. Despite great opposition and great turmoil everyone involved has grown closer in their relationships with Us." The Father rejoiced.

"Each response by someone who loves Us brought Me great joy during their trial and tribulations. Nothing the enemy has done created the results he expected. Now we've shown Lorraine Our love. The decision and confession are hers to decide. Now, We wait."

Noise from a host of angels drowned out the words of the Lord. Dancing, singing and rejoicing broke out in every corridor, nook and cranny of the heavenly realm. The Son smiled. Every angelic being gave God glory.

"A soul was just welcomed into the Kingdom. Things the enemy did to ruin them and work against them as evil, I turned for their good." The Father smiled at the Son. "The prayers of the righteous delivered great results. We've added all of the souls we scheduled to increase the Kingdom Of Heaven at this time."

"I prayed Lorraine wouldn't stay caught up in the tricks and traps set by the enemy but her resistance was so great I understood why the intercessors assigned to her wanted to give up a few times. I'm glad they continued to pray and take care of their assignment instead of accepting being exhausted and missing their reward. Now we can give them more than they can ever ask for, imagine or think." The Son said.

"This soul will be a great loss to the enemy. Her testimony and deliverance will save and set many others free. We will continue to love her and express how important she is to Us until she is perfect in whom We created her to be."

***

The bailiff opened the door to the judge's chambers. Judge Light nodded. He took his seat. "You may be seated."

"Judge Lorraine Allen, please stand." Judge Light looked at Tristan and Lorraine. "Over the course of this case one thing is clear. You were at some point caught in a precarious position while serving as an officer of the court. Based on the evidence presented I'm hesitant to pursue prosecution of Judge Lorraine Allen for abuse of power unless everyone whose presented the case against her can prove they did not participate in 'The Circle' as well."

Tears rolled down Lorraine's cheek so fast she couldn't catch them.

Tristan passed her the handkerchief from his breast pocket.

"I admonish you, Judge Allen to take careful consideration of the company you keep if you intend to continue serving as an officer of the court. Several people have spoken highly of your work in the community. A good reputation is not to be mistaken for being of good character. The person you are when you're alone and behind closed doors is the person you'll answer for being when this life is over. Your law clerk, Ms. Terry Johnson, expressed a profound respect and admiration for you as a mentor and friend. Please focus more on the relationships that will add to your life and not those which may cost more than they appear to require at their onset."

Lorraine nodded and wiped the tears from her face.

"Prosecutor Scribner, it is the official ruling of this court that insufficient evidence was presented and it is my ruling that we do not pursue prosecution. Furthermore, you should be aware all findings and evidence is being turned over to the State Prosecutor regarding the bribe and other falsified evidence presented. A woman of your intelligence and reputation should know to check facts better. That is all. Case dismissed." Judge Light banged his gavel.

***

Lorraine and Tristan stood outside of the courtroom.

"Can we go by my office to talk?" Lorraine smiled. "I missed saying that. My office."

Tristan nodded.

"I'll meet you there, just need to stop somewhere first." Lorraine patted him on the forearm. She took quick steps toward Terry when Scribner blocked her path.

"I know you think you won. This isn't over, Lorraine. As soon as I start things up again, we'll get you removed from office." Scribner crossed her arms.

"You know what, Scribner," Lorraine took a deep breath. She exhaled. "Helena, I'll never be able to convince you it wasn't personal so I'll quit trying. I don't like women despite my brief curiosity and cognac driven lapse in judgment at the cabin, I'm attracted to men, nothing will change that. Do whatever you want."

Scribner opened her mouth to respond and for a brief moment Lorraine could have sworn she saw a stone drop from her hands when no words came out.

Lorraine turned and walked toward Terry. "Terry ...Terry, I'm so sorry to put you and your son through all of this, please forgive me."

"There is no need to apologize, Judge. You didn't do anything wrong. They said you were not guilty." Terry hugged Lorraine. "The only thing I've ever needed to say since the day I met you in the Florida Women's Correctional Facility is thank you. I owe you for calling in those favors for Terrance. I think I'll send him to a different school next year. He liked being home with my mother so I'm looking into online public school. God has a mysterious way of working things out."

"You know Terry ... Never mind. I'll see you at the office." Lorraine smiled. "I can't tell you how good it feels to say that. Tristan is waiting for me there."

Lorraine took the stairs to her office. Tristan sat on the bench outside the door. She unlocked the door. The smell of the old law books and cherry wood felt like coming home.

"You really love practicing law." Tristan said. He sat in the high back chair in front of Lorraine's desk.

Lorraine nodded.

"Well, you want to tell me what really happened? The Circle, Helena Scribner and Ms. Terry Johnson?" Tristan said.

"Truth is, I did belong to 'The Circle'. I'm not ashamed or proud of it. However, I think I'll take Judge Light's advice and stay as far away from those people as possible. Once my appointment to the court is over, I may go back to practicing private law, or teach. I'm not sure. Everything is the same, but it feels different." Lorraine looked into Tristan's eyes. Her voice dropped several decibels. "I've never met anyone like you. Most men, married or single don't resist my advances.

No lawyer I know prays before trial. What is with you?"

"God told me to represent you in this case when I saw it on television. To be honest, I've followed your career since law school but I never knew you weren't a believer. Because of your social justice stances, community involvement and reputation I assumed you were a Christian. Christ came back for people like you and I. He died for our sins, so we could be reconciled with our heavenly Father. He is the one who acquitted you. I didn't know how He would, but I knew He would do it." Tristan laughed. "When I met you, I believed you were innocent. Once God and you revealed that was not true I wanted to walk away from the case, but God told me He would exonerate you and that He wanted to increase you. He allowed all of this to happen because He could never get your attention. There are others connected to you who believe in God but they were never able to distract you from your ambitions. Good people are just that, good people. This case, you, taught me even good people have habits and lifestyles behind closed doors that keep them far from God. He doesn't want to be far from you, Judge Allen.

Lorraine, Christ died on the cross for all of us including you and today He is knocking on the door of your heart, offering you a new life, an opportunity to know the God who delivered you from your enemies."

Tears rolled down Lorraine's cheeks. "What do I need to do? If He did all of this just to knock on my heart and I hear him, I want to let him in."

Tristan took the Judge's hand and led her through the sinner's prayer and into salvation.

***

Eternity the Throne of Grace

A loud yell echoed in heaven, "Noooo." Satan approached the throne furious. "Why? Why can't I win? She was a filthy woman doing perverted things and You still accepted her cry. Why?" Satan's head dropped.

"You're right. She was filthy, but I just cleansed her from all her unrighteousness and I have forgiven her of all her sins. Here is the thing, Satan; you desire to have permanently what you do not own. You asked for permission and I granted it to you. You don't even get it. I own, created, and control everything including you, snake. So understand this, whenever I give you entry to what I created, your time is always limited and comes with restricted access. Now leave My presence," the Father said with authority.

Satan removed himself quickly as instructed.

***

The Actual Event

At dawn, He appeared again in the temple courts, where all the people gathered around Him, and He sat down to teach them. The teachers of the law and the Pharisees brought in a woman caught in adultery. They made her stand before the group and said to Jesus, "Teacher, this woman was caught in the act of adultery. In the Law Moses commanded us to stone such women. Now what do you say?" They were using this question as a trap, in order to have a basis for accusing Him.

But Jesus bent down and started to write on the ground with His finger. When they kept on questioning Him, He straightened up and said to them, "Let any one of you who is without sin be the first to throw a stone at her." Again He stooped down and wrote on the ground.

At this, those who heard, began to go away one at a time, the older ones first, until only Jesus was left, with the woman still standing there. Jesus straightened up and asked her, "Woman, where are they who accuse you? Has no one condemned you?"

"No one, sir," she said.

"Then neither do I condemn you," Jesus declared. "Go now and leave your life of sin." *John 8:2-11 (NIV)*

###

Final Word From The Author

Some may say this book has gone to far because of some of the words used and all of the sexual information. But the truth is, God will go as far as He needs to in order to reach that person that may find themselves in Lorraine's position. Why do so many believers sit back and refuse to deal with the reality of our world? Many are afraid to stand with the accused especially when the accusation goes against what we believe. The bible tells us that the enemy is the accuser. His whole goal is to bring things up against you that will either disqualify you or cause others to view you differently. I want you to know that there is nothing that the enemy can accuse you of that will make God abandon you. Friends may leave, co-workers may stop talking to you, and family may disconnect from you, but the Lord will never leave you nor forsake you.

You must understand that maybe your sin is not a sexual one, maybe it's stealing. Whatever it is, you need to know that Jesus is looking at your life and is willing to represent you. The Lord is our Tristan – that even though He knows we are guilty, He keeps on arguing our case. Even though we continue to lie about where we are, The Lord keeps trying to reach us.

What I love about Jesus – our Lawyer and Defender – is that no matter what the sin is in your life, He is more focused on getting us to a free state where we leave what we are guilty of behind. Too many times, people try to cover up their truth instead of acknowledging it and moving forward. Like the woman caught in the act in John 8. She could have said to Jesus, "It wasn't me, Jesus. I didn't do what they are saying, Jesus. It was a mistake, or Jesus, I did it with my accusers, too." But she didn't. This lady stands there and goes through the process. Let me tell you, if you are still standing in the middle of your test and trial, that is enough to thank God for, because your standing through, will always speak louder than your excuse. Sometimes, those who accuse you, were once for you and the reason they have turned against you, is because you have moved on without them.

Let me encourage you. Jesus is for you, but not for your sin. Let today be a day where you look back over your life and see all the people who had stones in their hands ready to throw at you, but the Lord defended you and they dropped them. Look at all the times your sin could have gotten you in trouble, but your Tristan stood with you. Don't let your sin get you caught up in a scandal that only the Lord can get you out of. Like Jesus said, "I don't condemn, but leave your life of sin and sin no more." Remember, what the enemy meant for evil, God will turn around for good!

About The Author

Marquis Boone is a pastor, motivational speaker, author, entrepreneur and spiritual advisor to a host of celebrities. He is the Lead Pastor of Fresh Start Church which exists to revive, refresh, release and restore people back to God. Marquis Boone holds a Master of Arts in Christian Leadership and Masters of Divinity from Luther Rice University.

At the age of fourteen, Marquis Boone was licensed as a minister in his hometown, Baltimore, MD. He finished high school in two and a half years, graduating at the age of sixteen. By the age of nineteen Marquis completed his first degree Bachelor of Science in Business Administration with a minor in management. His gift has made room for him before more than a hundred thousand people throughout the world speaking across North America and in Europe. Marquis Boone has been a guest speaker at Bishop I.V. Hilliard Spiritual Encounter and Bishop T.D. Jakes MegaFest just to name a few. Marquis Boone resides in Georgia with his family. If you are ever in the Atlanta area he would love to see you at Fresh Start Church where he strives each day to make Jesus famous. www.myfreshstartchurch.org

twitter:@Boonem   www.marquisboone.com